"So Are You A Skilled Lover, Marc?"

Marc couldn't ignore Kate's query. He couldn't ignore her simple black pants and plain white blouse that would be easy to remove. "I don't make it a habit to speculate on my skill," he said.

"Maybe I should judge for myself."

"You have no idea what you're asking, Kate."

"I know exactly what I'm asking, Mark, and so do you. Does your expertise live up to the hype? If so, can you prove it to me?"

Propelled by his weakness for this woman, Marc closed the distance between them and sought her mouth in a rush, as if he couldn't survive without exploring the territory once more. She opened to him, played her tongue against his, pushed him to a point where he could easily dispense with all formality and clothing to get inside her.

After breaking the kiss, he settled his face in the hollow below her throat, pressing his lips there while inhaling her enticing fragrance.

"Marc, I thought you said we couldn't." Her voice was a breathy caress at his ear.

"Shouldn't," he murmured, then kissed the cleft between her breasts.

Dear Reader,

Welcome to another passion-filled month at Silhouette Desire. Summer may be waning to a close, but the heat between these pages is still guaranteed to singe your fingertips.

Things get hot and sweaty with Sheri WhiteFeather's *Steamy Savannah Nights,* the latest installment of our ever-popular continuity DYNASTIES: THE DANFORTHS. *USA TODAY* bestselling author Beverly Barton bursts back on the Silhouette Desire scene with *Laying His Claim,* another fabulous book in her series THE PROTECTORS. And Leanne Banks adds to the heat with *Between Duty and Desire,* the first book in MANTALK, an ongoing series with stories told exclusively from the hero's point of view. (Talk about finally finding out what he's *really* thinking!)

Also keeping things red-hot is Kristi Gold, whose *Persuading the Playboy King* launches her brand-new miniseries, THE ROYAL WAGER. You'll soon be melting when you read about Brenda Jackson's latest Westmoreland hero in *Stone Cold Surrender.* (Trust me, there is nothing cold about this man!) And be sure to *Awaken to Pleasure* with Nalini Singh's superspicy marriage-of-convenience story.

Enjoy all the passion inside!

Melissa Jeglinski

Melissa Jeglinski
Senior Editor
Silhouette Desire

Please address questions and book requests to:
Silhouette Reader Service
U.S.: 3010 Walden Ave., P.O. Box 1325, Buffalo, NY 14269
Canadian: P.O. Box 609, Fort Erie, Ont. L2A 5X3

PERSUADING THE PLAYBOY KING

KRISTI GOLD

Silhouette®

Desire

Published by Silhouette Books

America's Publisher of Contemporary Romance

SILHOUETTE BOOKS

ISBN 0-373-76600-9

PERSUADING THE PLAYBOY KING

Copyright © 2004 by Kristi Goldberg

Visit Silhouette Books at www.eHarlequin.com

Printed in U.S.A.

Books by Kristi Gold

Silhouette Desire

Cowboy for Keeps #1308
Doctor for Keeps #1320
His Sheltering Arms #1350
Her Ardent Sheikh #1358
*Dr. Dangerous #1415
*Dr. Desirable #1421
*Dr. Destiny #1427
His E-Mail Order Wife #1454
The Sheikh's Bidding #1485
*Renegade Millionaire #1497
Marooned with a Millionaire #1517
Expecting the Sheikh's Baby #1531
Fit for a Sheikh #1576
†Persuading the Playboy King #1600

*Marrying an M.D.
†The Royal Wager

KRISTI GOLD

has always believed that love has remarkable healing powers and feels very fortunate to be able to weave stories of romance and commitment. As a bestselling author and a Romance Writers of America RITA® Award finalist, she's learned that although accolades are wonderful, the most cherished rewards come from personal stories shared by readers.

You can reach Kristi at KGOLDAUTHOR@aol.com, through her Web site at www.kristigold.com or snail-mail at P.O. Box 9070, Waco, Texas, 76714. (Please include an SASE for a response).

To my incredible editor, Patience Smith,
for believing in this series.

Special acknowledgment goes to
Geoffrey and Lisa Buie-Collard for pushing me beyond
high school French. And to their niece, Dorian,
for inspiring a fantastical country.

Prologue

Prince Marcel Frederic DeLoria had a fondness for fast cars and the freedom he enjoyed while executing hairpin turns on winding roads. Yet his greatest pleasure came in the form of more dangerous curves, those that could be found on a woman. He appreciated every nuance of the opposite sex—the way they looked, the way they smelled, their innate intelligence and, admittedly, the challenges they could present when it came to the chase.

But as much as he loved women, he hated goodbyes and for that reason he'd avoided emotional entanglements. Still, tonight an inevitable parting hung over him like a guillotine, poised to sever ties four years in the making.

A few hours ago, Marc had taken his Harvard diploma and was now set to embrace his independence. However, he did not particularly look forward to saying goodbye to Sheikh Dharr Halim, in line to rule his country one day, and Mitchell Edward Warner III, the son of a United States senator and

American royalty in his own right. Three men bound by status, united by all that their legacies entailed, forever joined by a friendship that had grown and strengthened during their time together.

Noisy revelry filtered through the closed door from outside, a celebration signaling the end of an era, the end of their youth in a manner of speaking. The trio had opted to forgo the party and instead sequestered themselves in their shared apartment where they had formed their own fraternity of sorts, spending the past four years discussing culture, world events and their latest adventures skirting the ever-present paparazzi. And their favorite subject—women.

But tonight an uncharacteristic silence prevailed, as if the time-honored topics were inconsequential in light of what now awaited them—a future that no one could predict beyond their families' expectations.

Marc reclined on the black overstuffed chair, his heels propped on the table before him. Dharr sat regally in the tan leather lounger across from Marc, the traditional Arabian kaffiyeh no longer covering his head; yet he still gave the appearance of a born leader. Mitch had opted for his customary roost on the floor reclined against the wall, dressed in jeans and scuffed leather cowboy boots, apparel that stood out from the crowd like a crown on a pauper. But although they were all different, Marc acknowledged, they still shared notoriety, the reason behind their frequent gatherings, a means to cope with the pressures of celebrity.

Mitch tossed aside the magazine he'd been reading since their arrival and picked up the bottle of fine French champagne, compliments of Marc's brother, the king. "We've already toasted our success. Now I suggest we toast a long bachelorhood." He refilled his glass, then topped off Dharr's and Marc's.

Dharr raised his flute. "I would most definitely toast to that."

With champagne in hand, Marc paused to consider an idea—an appropriate send-off. One that would pique his friend's interests. "I prefer to propose a wager."

Dharr and Mitch glanced at one another then leveled their gazes on Marc. "What kind of wager, DeLoria?" Mitch asked.

"Well, since we've all agreed that we're not suited for marriage in the immediate future, if ever, I suggest we hold ourselves to those terms by wagering we'll all be unmarried on our tenth reunion."

"And if we are not?" Dharr asked.

Marc saw only one way to ensure the wager's success. "We'll be forced to give away our most prized possession."

"Give away my gelding?" Mitch grimaced as if he'd swallowed something foul. "That would be tough."

Dharr looked even less enthusiastic as his gaze fell on the abstract painting of a woman hanging above Mitch's head. "I suppose that would be my Modigliani original, and I must admit that giving away the nude would cause me great suffering."

"That's the point, gentlemen," Marc said. "The wager would mean nothing if the possessions were meaningless."

Mitch eyed him with suspicion. "Okay, DeLoria. What's it going to be for you?"

Marc thought only a moment before adding, "The Corvette."

"You'd give up the love mobile?" Mitch sounded incredulous.

"Of course not. I won't lose." And he wouldn't, because Marc DeLoria hated losing anything of worth.

"Nor will I," Dharr stated. "Ten years will be adequate before I am forced to adhere to an arranged marriage in order to produce an heir."

"No problem for me," Mitch said. "I'm going to avoid marriage at all costs."

Again Dharr held up his glass. "Then we are all agreed?"

Mitch touched his flute to Dharr's and Marc's. "Agreed."

Modern-day musketeers entering into an all-for-one pact. Marc raised his glass. "Let the wager begin."

Marc had no qualms about the ante. He could most definitely resist the temptation of a woman bent on tying him to an uneventful existence. He had no reason to marry, nor was he bound by duty to do so. Only one thing would be as unappealing to Marc as marriage—leading his country. But thanks to his birth order, Prince Marcel Frederic DeLoria would never have to suffer the fate of becoming king.

One

Nine years later

Marcel Frederic DeLoria had become a king.

Kate Milner had known him only as Marc, a seriously charming young man. A seriously inept biology student by his own admission, the reason why Kate had tutored him their freshman year at Harvard. And now he was the ruler of Doriana, a small European country.

Incredible.

Of course, the fact that she was standing in a storybook castle thousands of miles from home, preparing to see him again almost a decade later, seemed highly improbable, too. That made Kate smile.

But her smile immediately dissolved when he appeared at the end of the ornate palace foyer, a starched and polished middle-aged gentleman at his side. The mirrored walls, reflecting bursts of light from the crystal chandeliers, seemed to shrink as he drew closer, his confidence and calculated control almost palpable, even at a distance. His hair was still the same golden brown, somewhat longer than before, Kate realized, the fine layers windswept away from his face. Although he stood only slightly over six feet tall, he seemed more imposing now than when she'd known him before, with a broader chest and equally broad shoulders encased in a short-sleeved, form-fitting navy knit shirt that enhanced the considerable bulk of his biceps. He also wore a pair of faded jeans that outlined his narrow hips and solid thighs—the kind of clothes he'd worn in college, much to Kate's surprise. He was, after all, nobility.

Good grief. Had she really expected him to be decked out in a jewel-encrusted crown and red velvet robe? That he would be clutching a scepter instead of a pair of sunglasses? Silly that she would even consider such a thing. But she'd expected he at least would be wearing an expensive suit, not attire that could be found in a chic women's magazine ad extolling the virtues of cosmopolitan casual on hard-body hunks. Not that she was complaining.

When he came to a stop a few feet away, Kate was suddenly gripped by the sheer power of his presence, her pulse accelerating in response. She clung tightly to her composure when she contacted his piercing cobalt blue eyes—eyes that no longer held the mirth she had often witnessed during their previous time together. She saw something there that she couldn't quite peg. She also sensed an edge about him, a definite change that went far beyond the physical aspects.

One thing Kate did know, he gave no indication whatsoever that he recognized her. But why should he? Kate had changed, too, hopefully for the better.

The attendant took a brusque step forward and executed a slight bow. "Dr. Milner, I am Bernard Nicholas, His Majesty's primary aide."

Kate had the illogical urge to salute—or curtsy. She opted for a smile. "A pleasure to meet you."

Mr. Nicholas turned his attention to the silent, stoic king. "Your Majesty, may I present Dr. Katherine Milner, our latest candidate for the hospital position."

Marc moved forward and extended his hand, which Kate took after a slight hesitation. "Welcome to Doriana, Dr. Milner, and please forgive my appearance. I wasn't given much notice in regard to your arrival."

His voice sounded much the way Kate remembered, European sophisticated and distinctly seductive, only deeper. Yet he didn't look at all pleased, didn't even hint at a smile. In fact, his courtesy seemed almost forced. Considering the early hour, and his unshaven face, she couldn't help but wonder if maybe he'd just left the company of a woman, quite possibly a woman's bed.

His extracurricular activities shouldn't concern her. Yet the feel of his large masculine fingers wrapped around hers brought about a keen sense of awareness, the kind of awareness that came when confronted with a man she had been far too fond of. But Marc DeLoria was no ordinary man; he never had been. And obviously he had no recollection of their time together.

Kate decided he simply needed a reminder. "It's very nice to see you again, *Your Majesty.*"

He released her hand and frowned, fine lines deepening at the corners of his eyes, but they didn't detract from his magnificent face. "Have we met before?"

"Actually, the last time we were together, we were dissecting a deceased frog."

Confusion worked its way into his sedate expression followed by a fleeting glimpse of the carefree charmer she had once known. "Katie? The tutor?"

Kate's gaze faltered for a brief moment as she became the circumspect girl again. She forced away that notion, forced herself to look at him straight on. "Yes, that's me. Katie, the tutor. But I prefer Kate now. Or Dr. Milner, if that's more acceptable considering your current circumstance."

"My current circumstance?"

He actually had to be reminded of that, too? "You're a king."

"Ah, yes. That circumstance." He stared at her for a long moment, as if he couldn't quite believe she was there. Kate couldn't quite believe it, either.

After a bout of awkward silence, she finally said, "It's been a while, hasn't it?"

"Yes, quite a while." Although his smile had yet to form, he at least looked a little less perplexed when he gestured to a nearby room. "Shall we conduct the interview in the library, Doctor?"

Obviously he had no intention of taking a walk down memory lane. "Of course."

When Marc stepped to one side of the room's entry, Kate passed by him and caught a whiff of fresh air and fragrant cologne—clean, expensive, heavenly. Even though she shouldn't react so strongly, he still made her breathless. She'd always been that way to some degree in his presence.

Gathering her wits, Kate slowly turned around to survey the mahogany shelves lining the room. "This is quite a collection of books."

"My mother's favorites." He indicated a small settee near the window. "Please, have a seat."

Kate slid onto the green brocade sofa while Marc took the burgundy wingback chair across from her. When Mr. Nicholas positioned himself near the now-closed door, Marc told him, "That will be all."

The man stood steadfastly in place like a sentry, shoulders square, feet slightly apart, hands behind his back. "Beg pardon, but I believe it would be best if I remained, considering our guest is a lady."

"This is not the eighteenth century, Mr. Nicholas. You are dismissed."

"The Queen Mother—"

"Would understand the need for privacy."

"But—"

"I assure you that Dr. Milner's virtue is not in peril." Marc turned his attention to Kate. "Would you prefer not to be alone with me?"

She shrugged. "I don't see it as a problem at all. It certainly wouldn't be the first time." She secretly hoped it wouldn't be the last.

Marc sent another warning look at the attendant. "Tell Madame Tourreau to bring Dr. Milner some refreshments."

"As you wish, Your Reverence," Mr. Nicholas said, then took his leave.

Kate turned her attention to Marc, who looked anything but pleased. "Your Reverence?"

"Please ignore Mr. Nicholas. He's been with the family for quite some time and he has a penchant for making up titles. You should be flattered, though. Normally he doesn't do this around strangers, unless he feels they might appreciate his extremely dry and somewhat annoying British sense of humor."

"Oh, I see. It's sort of a game between you two."

"One game I would prefer not to play."

Kate could only imagine the games he did like to play—sensual games—and she really wouldn't mind playing them with him.

Business, Kate. No games, just business.

Marc crossed his legs at the ankles, his elbows resting on the chair's arms, hands clasped across his midsection. "So tell me, Dr. Milner, how did you discover we're seeking physicians in Doriana?"

Kate toyed with her hem, surprisingly drawing Marc's gaze. Considering her disheveled state, he probably wondered if the royal cat had dragged her across the regal doorstep. Her lavender silk suit showed creases resulting from hours of travel. Her hair had lost every bit of its curl and now hung down in board-straight strands to her shoulders. When his gaze came to rest on her mouth, she assumed she had a pink lipstick smear across her teeth.

Kate resisted the urge to run a finger over her incisors. "I saw the story in the alumni newsletter, right after your coronation," she said, pulling his attention back to her eyes. "You mentioned that your first order of business involved recruiting doctors, so I contacted the hospital, and now here I am. By the way, I was very sorry to hear about your brother's car accident."

She saw a flash of sadness in his eyes before it vanished as quickly as it had come. "Did you attend medical school at Harvard?"

Considering his swift change of subject, Kate made a mental note not to bring up his brother's death again. "Actually, I returned home to Tennessee and went to Vanderbilt. I needed to be close to my family."

"Was someone ill?" he asked with concern.

"Not really." Only needy, and very overprotective as always, which was one of the reasons why Kate had decided to apply for the position—the other was sitting before her. She'd grown tired of being the perfect, reliable daughter—the person both her parents depended upon for everything. She loved them dearly, but at times she wished she'd had siblings to ease some of her burden.

Marc crossed his arms over his chest, looking commanding and no less sexy. "You say you needed to be close to your family yet you have traveled thousands of miles away to work in our hospital?"

"I've been looking for a change of pace." A change of scenery. A change in her life.

"What is your medical specialty?" he asked in an all-business tone, confirming that he was only interested in the interview.

"Family practice," she said. "But I enjoy treating children the most. I've always loved children."

"They're our hope for future generations," he replied. "We've made some strides in pediatric health care, but not enough for my satisfaction."

"I'd enjoy that challenge, Marc. I mean, Your Highness." Her first breach of royal protocol, and probably not her last. "I'm sorry."

"No apology necessary, Dr. Milner."

"I really prefer you call me Kate. I'm just a simple kind of person."

"But you're also a physician," he said. "Not many can lay claim to that."

Kate felt the bloom of a blush on her cheeks. She'd never been well versed in accepting flattery graciously, but then compliments hadn't been a common occurrence in her life. "Speaking of doctors, how soon do you plan to reach a decision on who you'll be hiring?"

"The decision will come when we find the right candidate. And on that thought, could you tell me about your experience?"

"Exactly what experience are you referring to?" How could she have asked such a stupid question? Easy. The man was sucking her brain dry of lucid thought with his high-powered aura.

She noted a spark of amusement in his eyes and the first signs of a smile, but not enough to reveal the dimples framing his mouth. "Medical experience, of course. Unless you have other experience that you believe might interest me."

If only that were true. "Medically speaking, I've only recently completed my residency. I haven't been in private practice at all."

His dark gaze pinned her in place, even though she wanted to fidget. "I assume you've been adequately trained."

She lifted her chin a notch. "In one of the top programs in the country."

"Then I would say you could handle our hospital clinic."

"I'm sure I could." Now for the nitty-gritty. "And the pay?"

Marc leaned forward, bringing with him another trace scent of cologne. "If we come to an agreement, I would be willing to match whatever salary you were making in the States."

"Believe me, my salary barely enabled me to make ends meet. Long hours, low pay. I still have some student loans to take care of."

"I could at least double it," he said. "More if necessary."

This deal was getting sweeter by the minute. "Why would you do that?"

"Because we are in need of good doctors. And after all, we're old friends."

"Lab partners," she corrected. "I never really considered us friends."

He leaned back, but kept his eyes fixed on hers. "Why is that, Kate?"

"That's fairly obvious, considering you're a king and I'm, well, me."

"But when we knew each other before, I wasn't a king."

And she'd been far removed from royalty. She still was. "No, you were a prince. I was never all that comfortable around you because of that."

"Do I still make you uncomfortable?" he asked in a deep, deadly voice that held both challenge and temptation.

Very. "Not really. I've had interviews before. I consider this opportunity an adventure."

"Then I'm to assume you're looking for adventure?"

"And a job."

"We have the job covered. So what type of adventure are you looking for, aside from your career?"

The question hung in the air for a time until she finally said, "I'm not sure. Do you have any suggestions?"

The dark look he sent her said he probably had plenty. "Unfortunately, Doriana is a rather sedate place in July. But if you're here during the winter season, you could take advantage of our ski resorts. We have some challenging slopes, if you're not afraid to attempt something that could be deemed dangerous."

Now why had that sounded like an invitation to sin? "I've never tried skiing, but it sounds like fun."

"I wouldn't object to teaching you as repayment for what you taught me. I doubt I would have passed biology had it not been for you."

She certainly wouldn't object to anything he wanted to teach her. "Are you good?" *Great, Kate.* "At skiing, I mean."

His eyes seemed to grow even darker, effectively dispensing the last of Kate's calm. "Yes."

"I imagine you're probably very good at everything you do." Imagined it in great detail, she did. "Aside from biology, that is."

"I would imagine the same applies to you, Kate, considering how well you handled me during that first year."

She made a shaky one-handed sweep through her hair. "Funny, I don't remember handling you at all."

He assumed an almost insolent posture, his gaze now centered on her lap where she ran her fingertips up and down her purse strap. "Well, if you had *literally* handled me, I would not have forgotten, I assure you."

If he only knew how many times she'd imagined "handling" him in her wildest fantasies. How many times she had imagined this moment when they were again face-to-face. How strongly she was reacting to him on a very primal level.

Following a brief span of tense silence, reality finally drilled its way into Kate's psyche. She could not let him get to her again. Not this time. All those years ago, she had fallen hopelessly in love with him, knowing he could never feel the same—a mistake she didn't dare repeat.

But that was then, and this was now. She had matured beyond the point of having puppy-love crushes on unattainable men. She had only fond feelings for Marc DeLoria.

Okay, maybe fond wasn't a good assessment. She was unequivocally ready to jump his aristocratic bones. But she wouldn't.

Marc DeLoria was a dynamic king, a magnetic man. And from all news accounts, he was also a rounder, a rogue and one of the world's most notorious playboys. She needed to remember that—even if she was still seriously attracted to him, whether she wanted to be or not.

Kate tried to appear nonchalant when her overheated body was anything but unfazed by his continued perusal. "Anything else you need to know about me?"

"There is something I would like to do with you, if you're not too tired from your trip."

Her heart rate did double time. "What would that be?"

"Show you the hospital, as soon as I change into something more appropriate."

Darn. For a split second, Kate had hoped he was going to propose something more exciting. "I would really like to see the facilities."

"And I see no reason why the position could not be yours if you so choose."

She frowned. "Just like that?"

He rubbed a hand along his shaded jaw. "Frankly, you've already been highly recommended by the hospital's administrator. Our meeting is only a formality."

"I'll definitely consider your offer," she said. "But first I'd like to take a look around and make sure it's the right place for me."

"Speaking of that, do you have a place to stay?"

"I have a room at the St. Simone Inn."

"You should stay at the palace as our guest. You would be much more comfortable here."

No, she wouldn't. Not with him occupying the same castle, even if it did have a hundred rooms, which she suspected it did. "I appreciate your hospitality, but I would prefer the inn."

"Please let me know if you change your mind." His voice had the appeal of hot buttered rum, rich and warm going down.

"I sure will." Her voice sounded a little too down-home with a too-high pitch.

After a brief knock, a stout, gray-haired woman breezed into the room with a tray of tea and cookies. She kept her eyes averted as she served Kate first.

Marc declined the tea, but after the woman retreated, he took one of the treats and held it to her lips. "Try the *rollitos*. They're Spanish cookies, one of my two favorite indulgences."

She wasn't sure she could swallow. "Really? What would the other be?"

Marc's smile arrived slowly but it quickly impacted Kate's control at the first sign of his deep dimples. "A person should be allowed to have a few secrets, Kate. Even a king."

Kate bit into the cookie but she didn't taste a thing. Considering Marc's overt sensuality, she suspected he had a lot of secrets. She also suspected his other favorite indulgence had nothing to do with food and everything to do with his desires as a man. A man who was much too tempting for his own good. For Kate's own good.

Since his days at Harvard, Marcel DeLoria had spent almost eight years seeing the world and its wonders. For the past nine months, he had seen what it was like to have every molecule of his character examined as if he'd been placed under a high-powered microscope, not on the proverbial throne. But in all his experiences, he had never seen anything quite as surprising as the woman sitting across from him in the back seat of the Rolls-Royce.

Years before, he'd known her as a shy, intelligent student who had hidden behind too-big clothing and owl-like glasses, not the confident, stylish woman she had become. He admired her self-assurance as much as her physical conversion. And he definitely needed to quit admiring her altogether lest she catch him in the act.

As they continued through St. Simone en route to the hospital, Marc turned his attention to the quaint, colorful shops lining the cobblestoned streets. Streets practically void of automobile traffic, yet heavy with tourists and locals who had stopped to watch the motorcade pass. Would he ever grow accustomed to such spectacle? Probably not.

At times, he longed to walk among the villagers as an ordinary man, stop by the bakery and pick up his second-favorite indulgence—in terms of food—éclairs. At times, he craved putting on his old college sweatshirt and jeans to join in a game of rugby with the local team. At times, he wished he had never been born into royalty.

"This town is incredible, Your Highness."

The soft lilt of Kate's voice brought his attention back to her, brought to mind more of Marc's recollections of their time together. He remembered being enamored of its quiet charm—a southern accent, she had once told him. But he had never viewed her as more than a friend. And somewhat of a savior. Had it not been for her, he might never have finished that first grueling year at Harvard.

She pointed out the window. "What's that building over there?"

Against his better judgment, Marc moved to the seat beside her, maintaining a somewhat comfortable distance. "That is St. Simone Cathedral. My parents were married there."

She turned her incredible green eyes on his. "It's beautiful, all that stained glass."

"I tend to take the village for granted," he told her, striving for casual conversation when what he wanted to do with his mouth had nothing to do with talking.

"I guess that's understandable," she said. "Beauty is easy to overlook if you face it on a daily basis."

When she turned back to the window, Marc decided she was very beautiful as well. He supposed many would view her as merely cute, with her upturned nose, graced with a slight spattering of freckles, her rounded face, not the more striking, sharper features common among what some considered the world's greatest beauties. But her large eyes—a near match in color to the pines blanketing the Pyrenees—and her chestnut hair falling about her shoulders, were very pleasing attributes, in his opinion.

Although he tried to tear his gaze away from her, Marc found himself taking another visual excursion. The tailored lavender silk suit she wore fit her to prime perfection, showcasing a pair of elegant legs that would garner any man's attention. She was relatively small—small hands, small feet and best he could tell, not endowed with ample curves or breasts. But he'd always believed that some of the best things in life came in small parcels. He imagined Kate was no exception.

Even though he shouldn't, he saw her as attractive woman that he would like to know much better. Perhaps eventually in the tangle of warm satin sheets—not in the cold confines of a college laboratory. But that was impossible.

As much as the man in Marc desired Kate Milner, the king that he had become prevented him from acting on that desire. He must remain strong in light of his need to be taken seriously as his country's leader.

Still, it would be very easy to press the button on the console, raise the windowed partition separating them from the driver and Nicholas, and allow some privacy away from prying eyes.

A fantasy assaulted him then, sharp as shattered glass—images of sliding his mouth up her delicate throat, working his way to her lips and engaging her in a provocative kiss. In his mind, Kate would be receptive to his affections, encouraging him onward as he slipped his hand beneath the hem of her skirt, moving up, up until he touched her, first through damp silk, then beneath the barrier so he could experience her heat. He would tempt her with his fingers, tantalize her with his mouth and endeavor to make her moan, make her want him inside her. He would gladly comply without regard to who he was or where he was. Without consideration of the consequences. He would make love to her until they were both sated, if only temporarily...

The vehicle came to an abrupt halt, effectively splintering the images but not the results of Marc's journey into a wicked fantasy. He was hard as slate below his belt and could do nothing to hide his predicament short of grabbing a handful of ice from the built-in bar and shoving it into his lap. He only hoped that Kate would not notice before he had a chance to compose himself, and that his dress coat would amply conceal his sins once they exited the car.

Marc straightened his shoulders and assumed his royal demeanor while continuing to battle a strong desire for Kate Milner that made absolutely no sense. He wrote the libidinous stirrings off to a lengthy celibacy—a situation born out of necessity due to his brother's tragic death that had thrust Marc into the role of reluctant ruler.

He adjusted his tie, tugged at his collar and sent Kate a polite smile. "It seems we have reached our destination." And not a moment too soon. Otherwise, he might have forgotten who he was and what he lacked—a life he could call his own. A life that had no room for courting women, stealing kisses and touches or forbidden fantasies.

Seeming not to notice his discomfort, Kate glanced out the window at the simple two-story building. "It's a very nice hospital."

Marc detected a hint of disappointment in her tone, aiding somewhat in his body's return to decency. "It's very small and admittedly somewhat lacking in modern equipment. But I'm determined to remedy that soon."

Health care was of the utmost importance, not only to Marc but also to his people. Doriana needed better facilities, more doctors. Had the hospital been modernized, Philippe might still be alive, and Marc would still be feeding his wanderlust instead of attempting to prove himself.

Kate offered an understanding smile. "These things take time."

Marc couldn't agree more, but he felt as if he were running out of time.

When Nicholas opened the door, Marc took Kate's hand and helped her from the car. Her slender fingers cradled in his palm spurred another random fantasy that involved another pleasurable touch. How could he continue to be around her and still maintain control?

On sheer willpower alone.

But after Kate slid from the limo and his hand came to rest on her lower back, contacting the delicate dip of her spine encased in silk, Marc's willpower went the way of the wind, replaced by an instantaneous shock to his senses—one that he had to disregard in order to save face.

He focused on the substantial crowd that had gathered, held at bay by a contingent of bodyguards. As always, he was forced to play the royal role with a regal facade and an official smile. Kate paused at his side when he stopped to shake the hands of a few subjects. The crowd voiced their pleasure with applause and several women pointed, but not at him. They were pointing at Kate, whispering behind their hands.

Marc realized all too late that they mistakenly believed Kate to be his current paramour, understandable since he again had his palm firmly planted on her back.

Marc took a much-needed step away from Kate, but not before he was joined by Dr. Jonathan Renault—resident hospital irritant—who had worked his way through the chaos.

"Good day, Your Majesty," Renault said, his voice dripping with sarcasm.

Marc did not trust the man, and even less so when Renault blatantly assessed Kate from forehead to toes. "Good day, Dr. Renault," he said with strained civility.

When Marc tried to usher Kate away, Renault stopped him cold by saying, *"Je voudrais faire la connaissance de votre nouvelle petite amie."*

Petite amie. A direct intimation that Kate was Marc's mistress. And to add to his total lack of propriety, he'd had the nerve to request an introduction.

In another time, in another place, Marc would have gladly punished the bastard with a slam of a fist into Renault's prominent jaw. But Marc's title prevented what would be considered a crude, common act. Crude, yes. Common, yes. Unjustified? Not in Marc's opinion.

"For your information, Dr. Renault," Marc began, an intentional trace of venom in his tone, "this is Dr. Katherine Milner. She is a very skilled physician, and quite capable of managing the entire clinic by herself."

Although Kate looked somewhat confused, Renault didn't appear at all affected by the pointed comment. Instead, he sent Kate a seamy smile and took her hand. *"Enchanté,* Dr. Milner. I would be happy to have you join my staff."

Kate quickly pulled out of his grasp, giving Marc great satisfaction. Obviously she recognized the lecher beneath the lab coat. "Nice to meet you, Doctor," she said with little enthusiasm.

Renault winked. "And I will look forward to seeing you again."

With that, he strode away with a self-important lift of his pointy chin and a swaggering gait.

Kate leaned over until her lips were practically resting on Marc's ear. "What did he say to you?"

"Keep walking." Marc took her by the elbow and continued on to the hospital entry. Once they were on the steps, he lowered his voice and said, "He suggested we are lovers. A totally absurd assumption, but then Renault is somewhat lacking in restraint."

Yet Marc wondered if something in his own demeanor, the way he had looked at Kate, the way he'd touched her so casually, had encouraged the speculation, not only in Renault but also in the minds of his people.

If that were the case, he would have to be more careful from this point forward. He could not allow anyone to believe that he had taken Kate Milner as his lover, even if he longed to do that very thing.

Two

An absurd assumption...

Up to that point, Kate had allowed herself to imagine she was a real, live, honest-to-goodness princess greeting royal subjects with her prince, who'd kept touching her as if he wanted everyone to know she was his.

King, she reminded herself. A man who was obviously the object of desire to women of all shapes and sizes. A man who could have his pick among any woman in this village, probably in the world. She would never be among them. This wasn't a fairy tale, and this particular monarch wasn't interested in common Kate Milner.

But Dr. Renault had certainly seemed interested, and that consideration made Kate cringe. The guy gave her the creeps.

None of that mattered. She was here on business, not to worry about some dubious doctor with "I want you" written all over his face. Not to get caught up in some overblown forever-after fantasy involving a king who thought the idea of being her lover was absurd.

Forcing herself into professional mode, Kate followed behind Marc as they made their way to the hospital's entrance where two guards remained posted. When they entered the building, she was pleasantly surprised by the modern interior. The practically deserted waiting room, filled with contemporary chairs and tables as well as a television suspended from a stand in the corner near the ceiling, was much larger than she'd expected.

A sign positioned near the elevator written in French and Spanish indicated the location to various units. She knew some Latin, a few basic words in Spanish and only enough French to inquire about restaurants and rest rooms. She had brought along some books and tapes to study. But when treating patients, communication was a must. Maybe she would be making a mistake if she accepted the position, something she would definitely have to consider.

Kate followed Marc to the reception desk, where he presented a polite smile to the pleasant-looking older woman seated behind a computer.

A few moments later, an elderly, distinguished man with thinning gray hair pushed through the double doors to the right of the waiting area. He approached them with a wide smile. "Ah, Doctor Milner, I presume. I am Dr. Louis Martine, chief of medicine. We spoke briefly on the phone when you inquired about the position."

Kate extended her hand. "A pleasure to finally meet you, Dr. Martine."

He inclined his head and looked at her quizzically. "You truly have a unique accent."

Obviously her Deep South roots were still firmly wrapped around her tongue. "It's southern United States."

Dr. Martine smiled. "*Très charmant* to suit a *belle femme*."

"I'm sorry, I'm afraid I don't understand," Kate said.

"Very charming to suit a beautiful woman," Marc supplied, followed by an appreciative look that made Kate shiver.

She felt another blush spreading from her throat to her forehead and tried to will it away. Contacts instead of glasses, a new wardrobe and a good beautician might have changed her outward appearance, but it couldn't mask the plain, unassuming girl that lived inside. At times she still saw herself as too skinny, too short, too awkward, too lacking in social skills. So what was she doing here, in the presence of royalty?

Ludicrous. She was a doctor, and she'd worked too darned long to let insecurities derail her hard-earned self-confidence.

Marc made a sweeping gesture toward the double doors. "Shall we take the tour now?"

Kate followed Marc and Dr. Martine through a maze of hallways into a place resembling a clinic. This particular waiting room was full of mothers and fathers and children. When she detected the familiar sterile scents, she felt somewhat back in her element and relaxed.

They strode through another door where an attractive brunette nurse with huge blue eyes and large breasts eyed Marc as if he were today's special at Bennie's Diner. Marc ignored her furtive glances and guided Kate inside a small office.

"This would be your station should you decide to accept the position," Marc said.

Kate did a quick visual search and noticed the desk was cluttered with charts and coffee cups. "Whose office is this now?"

"Jonathan Renault, our current family practitioner," Dr. Martine said. "I'm afraid you will have to share the space with him until we can set up another office for you."

Oh, joy. Kate was not looking forward to that.

"And I assume you will be seeing to a private office for Dr. Milner immediately, Louis?" Marc stated in a firm tone.

"Of course, Your Highness," Martine replied. "It shouldn't

take more than a day or two should she decide to join our staff."

That remained to be seen. Kate had already come upon two very important challenges—the language barrier and the beast named Renault. Three if she considered her attraction to Marc.

Dr. Martine studied the stethoscope dangling from his neck. "Dr. Renault is a good *médecin,* but I am afraid he is not as interested in his practice and the patients as we would wish him to be."

Marc frowned. "I would say that is a grave understatement, Louis." He gave Kate a cynical look. "Renault is much more interested in the female staff. I have put him on notice that if I receive one more complaint, he will have to return to Paris."

"Oh," Kate said. "What hours does he work?" If luck prevailed, she could avoid him—if she decided to stay.

"Since the clinic is only open during the day, you would be working together," Martine said.

No luck there, Kate thought.

"If he becomes unmanageable, inform me," Marc added. "I will take care of him."

"I'm sure I can take care of myself," Kate insisted, mildly insulted that men tended to see women as the weaker sex. She might be small, but she knew where to thrust a knee on a strategic part of the male anatomy.

A rap came at the door and Nurse Lustful entered. She exchanged a few words with Dr. Martine, who then turned to Marc. "You have a call from the palace, Your Majesty. Line one."

After he uncovered the debris from the desk phone, Marc picked up the receiver. He again spoke words Kate couldn't begin to understand, but his distress was very apparent in his expression. Once he hung up, he turned to her and said, "We must return to the palace immediately. There's been an incident."

A serious incident, Kate presumed. "Should I stay here? Dr. Martine could show me around."

"I could possibly need your medical expertise."

Kate's concern increased. "Has someone been hurt?"

"Not exactly. But it does involve a child."

With Kate trailing behind him, Marc strode into the palace's formal parlor to find his mother seated on the settee, holding what appeared to be the reason for his urgent summons.

She nodded at the sleeping infant in her arms and said, "I do hope you can explain this to me, Marcel."

Explain? "It appears to be a child, Mother."

She rose with typical grace and laid the baby in Marc's arms, much to his dismay. "It appears to be your daughter, my son."

He heard the sound of Kate's sharp, indrawn breath from behind him. Unfortunately, Marc's respiration had halted altogether.

Once he'd recovered his voice, he said, "This is not my child."

The baby chose that moment to lift her head, turn an alarming shade of red and wail at the top of her lungs. Marc had no idea such a small creature could create such a furor. He also had no idea what to do when she began to writhe, except to hold on tightly lest he drop her. The tighter he held her, the more she wrestled and squirmed, arching her back against her confinement.

"Here, let me." Kate took the baby from him and positioned the child on her shoulder, patting her back. The infant immediately quieted, her sobs turning to sniffs.

Kate had rescued him once again, at least for now. He met his mother's disapproving expression. "Mother, I have no idea why you would believe this is my child."

She turned to her attendant, who stood in the corner looking as if she would greatly like to flee. "Beatrice, bring me the note."

The young woman hurried over and handed her a plain

piece of white paper. In turn, his mother handed it to him. "The baby was left at the gate in a pram with a bag full of clothing and bottles. We found this note inside."

Marc read it silently. The words were English, brief, but to the point.

"Her name is Cecile. She is a DeLoria."

Shoving the paper into his pocket, he said, "This does not prove a thing. It's obviously a ruse."

"Look at her, Marcel."

Marc turned to the baby now propped on Kate's hip, occupying herself with the button on Kate's jacket. True, she had his hair color and blue eyes, but that did not mean she was his. He had been careful to the extreme. He had not been involved with anyone since Elsa Sidleberg—an international supermodel who still graced renowned runways—and that had ended over a year ago. This made no sense whatsoever.

"Again, her appearance proves nothing," he insisted.

"Nor does it disprove anything," his mother replied.

Kate stepped forward. "Maybe I can help."

Marc realized that his mother and Kate had yet to be formally introduced. He supposed his lack of manners was understandable considering the circumstance. "Kate, I present to you the Queen Mother, Mary Elizabeth Darcy DeLoria. Mother, Dr. Kate Milner."

Kate smiled and held out her free hand. "It's very nice to meet you. I'm sorry, but how do I address you?"

She took Kate's hand for a brief shake. "I would prefer you call me Mary." She sent a sardonic glance at Marc. "Obviously, you now know the family secrets, so I believe first names are appropriate."

Marc clung to his last thin thread of control. "I have no secrets, Mother. And this is not my child."

Mary smoothed a hand over the baby's hair. "Then why

would anyone claim this precious girl is a DeLoria? What other possibilities are there?"

Marc knew of one, and he was taking great risk by mentioning it. But he felt he must. "Perhaps she is Philippe's child."

His mother sent him a startled look, as if he'd proclaimed that a deity had committed a mortal sin. "That would be impossible. Philippe has been gone for almost a year."

Marc turned to Kate. "How old do you think she is?"

Kate regarded the baby for a moment. "At least six months old, maybe a bit older if she's small for her age."

"It really doesn't matter," Marc said. "She could have been born before or shortly after Philippe's death. Definitely conceived while he was still alive."

"Philippe was engaged to marry Countess Jacqueline Trudeau for two years."

"Perhaps she is the mother, then."

"Nonsense. She married another man not long after Philippe's death."

Ah, true love, Marc thought cynically. "Then perhaps Philippe fathered a child with another woman."

"Philippe never would have denied his child," Mary said.

Anger welled inside Marc. "And I would?"

"As his mother, I would have known if he had been hiding something. He was never good at telling untruths. He lacked the cunning you have."

The woman who had always been Marc's champion had called him a practiced deceiver in front of Kate, a woman whose respect he greatly desired. "Are you saying I am prone to telling falsehoods?"

"I am saying you've always been more clever and not as easy to read."

"Of course. And Philippe was destined for sainthood." Marc could not keep the sarcasm and bitterness from his tone even though he, too, had admired his brother. But he had also lived in his shadow. He was still living in it.

His mother's expression softened. "My dear Marcel, we barely saw you over the past ten years, let alone knew with whom you were involved aside from what we read in the papers."

"And you knew of Philippe's comings and goings all the time, Mother? Might I remind you that no one knew where he was going or where he had been the night he died."

"I am deeply wounded by your suggestion that your brother was carrying on with someone I knew nothing about, much less had a child with that someone without my knowledge."

Kate watched the verbal volley as she continued to hold the baby on her hip, feeling totally like an outsider. The tension in the room was as thick as buttermilk and although she had no business getting involved, she had to do something. "There are ways to prove parentage," she offered.

Both Marc and his mother unlocked their gazes from each other and turned them to her.

"Perhaps a birthmark?" the queen mother asked in a hopeful voice. "Marc does have a very unusual one on his—"

"Mother, I believe Dr. Milner is referring to something more scientific."

Kate was, but she had to admit she was curious about Marc's royal birthmark and where it might be residing. "I'm referring to DNA, which is complicated if the testing can't be done here." Not to mention they would have to obtain some from the deceased brother, a fact she didn't dare bring up now.

Marc streaked a hand over his nape. "We are not up to speed with that yet. We would have to involve Paris."

"We cannot do that," the queen mother said, looking alarmed. "We must keep this concealed until we decide how to handle such a sensitive issue. The media would tear Marcel to shreds if they even suspected he had fathered a child out of wedlock. He would lose all respect in the eyes of our people."

Kate could understand that, and she was more than a bit concerned herself. "I could draw and type her blood but without knowing the mother's type, it might not tell us anything."

"My blood type is rare," Marc said. "Would that make a difference?"

"It could if she has it. That could prove she's a member of the family, but it still might not rule anyone out." She didn't want to ask, but she had to. "What about Philippe's type?"

"His was the same as Marc's," Mary said. "The night he died…" Mary's voice trailed off along with her gaze.

Marc released a gruff sigh. "My mother was about to say that the night he died, I was in Germany on a diplomatic mission. He suffered severe internal injuries in the car crash. He lost too much blood and I didn't arrive in time to give him some of my own."

Kate's heart went out to Marc in that moment. She couldn't think of anything to say to ease his guilt, so she said nothing.

"Dr. Martine can provide all the medical records since he's the royal physician," Mary said. "We can trust him to be discreet." She paused before adding, "And I assume we can trust you as well, Dr. Milner?"

Marc moved closer to Kate, a purely defensive gesture. "Mother, Kate is a physician. She is accustomed to confidentiality."

Mary arched a thin brow. "Kate? How well do you know each other?"

Oh, heavens. If she didn't set the record straight, the queen mother might assume she was Marc's lover. Worse, she might believe Kate had parental ties to the child considering the timing. "Actually—"

"Kate, forgive my mother. She might be descended from genteel British aristocracy, but she has the bluntness of a barrister pleading a monumental case."

The queen mother patted his cheek, a true display of fondness that took Kate by surprise in light of their recent confrontation. "And so do you, *mon fiston*."

"In case you haven't noticed, Mother, I am no longer your little boy."

"Yes, you are a man now and clearly responsible for your actions."

"Kate and I knew each other at the university," Marc continued, obviously not willing to react to the innuendo, much to Kate's relief. "I assure you that we have not seen each other in years."

"We were college lab partners," Kate interjected. "Only friends."

Finally, Marc smiled. "And she's come to Doriana to join our hospital staff."

The baby wriggled and gave a whine of protest. Kate wanted to do the same since she hadn't exactly agreed to take the job. "I think we should wait until morning to do the tests. She's been through enough today." *And so have I*, Kate thought.

The queen mother patted her neat silver chignon, her features mellowing when she smiled at Kate. "Welcome, my dear. We are very pleased to have you."

Kate considered insisting that she hadn't made her final decision, but with the queen mother and king looking at her expectantly, she felt as if she had no choice.

She would agree to take the position—for the time being. If it got too hot in the castle kitchen, if it turned out the baby was Marc's and he'd left some woman high and dry, alone and pregnant, she would have to reconsider. She couldn't respect a man who would do that, even if she did crave his company.

"Thank you. I'm very glad to be here."

For now.

Marc spent the remainder of the afternoon making numerous queries, only to learn that no one seemed to know who had delivered the baby at the gates. He called Louis Martine and explained the situation, then arranged to meet him early in the morning at the hospital for Kate to run the tests. Louis had assured him that he would practice prudence when it came to gathering records and assisting in trying to determine the baby's parentage. Marc had no choice but to trust him. He could not say the same for the rest of the hospital staff, Renault particularly, so they would have to proceed with caution.

Frustrated and exhausted, Marc set off to locate his mother and Kate, who had insisted on staying to care for the baby. Beatrice directed him up the stairs to what was once his and Philippe's nursery, but which had long ago been transformed into a guestroom. He entered to find Kate sitting in a rocker, holding the sleeping child against her shoulder. She put a fingertip to her lips as she rose and laid the little girl in the nearby crib. The baby stirred a bit and Kate remained there for a while, patting the child's back and cooing like a dove. After a time, she turned away and signaled him to join her in the hall.

Once there, she shut the door behind them and sighed. "I think she's finally down for the count. It took a while. Apparently she's used to someone rocking her to sleep."

Marc rubbed his neck, trying to work away the tension coiled there, to no avail. "I suspect her mother had that duty, whoever she might be."

"I'm sure you're right. And obviously Cecile's been well cared for. She looks very healthy. I'll do a full exam tomorrow, just to be sure."

Marc glanced at the closed door. "I'm surprised at how quickly you've made the room into a nursery again."

Kate shrugged. "I didn't do anything but play with Cecile while the staff moved in the furniture."

"My mother must have called in all her favors to have a crib delivered so quickly."

"The crib was yours."

"I had no idea my mother kept it."

"She obviously cares a great deal for you," Kate said softly.

Marc acknowledged that his mother had always cared about him, but after the events of the day, he questioned whether she respected him. "By the way, where is she?"

"She had a terrible headache so I insisted she go to bed. I'm sure it's stress."

No doubt due to the situation, and him. "I hope we clear this up soon. She's been through quite a lot over the past year with Philippe's death. And now this."

He saw true sympathy in Kate's emerald eyes. "Yes, she has been through a lot, and so have you."

How unselfish for her to consider his feelings, Marc thought. A rare occurrence in the household. "I've adjusted." He'd been forced to adjust. No time to consider anything but duty. No time to really grieve.

"Are you sure you've adjusted?" she asked.

No, he wasn't, yet the time to assess his situation would probably continue to elude him. "Of course."

Kate hid a yawn behind her hand. "I'm so sorry."

Marc felt like a selfish fool. "No apology necessary. You must be exhausted from your trip."

Her ensuing smile tripped Marc's pulse into a frenzy. "Yes, I am tired. Beatrice has agreed to sleep in the room adjacent to the nursery in case Cecile wakes during the night. Do you think Mr. Nicholas could drive me back to the hotel?"

Marc wasn't ready for her to leave. He wanted to spend more time with her even knowing it was selfish on his part, and totally ill-advised. "Are you certain you wouldn't like to stay here considering the lateness of the hour?"

"My clothes are at the hotel and I really need a bath."

Marc did not need to imagine her in the bath, but he did— in great detail, right down to the curve of her hip, the shading between her thighs, the roundness of her breasts where his gaze now came to rest.

Kate pointed to a dark smudge above her right breast. "Strained peas. Little Cecile is a healthy eater but she loves to toss food. Her aim is pretty darned good."

Marc reached for a lock of Kate's dark hair. "Yes, I do believe I see a few remnants here."

As he twined the soft strands in his fingers, their gazes remained fixed as Kate said, "I'm only a phone call away if you need anything."

Marc needed something from her now—although he couldn't act on that need. He dropped his hand and stepped back. "I will personally see to your return. I'll drive you myself."

Her expression reflected wariness. "Are you sure? You look pretty beat."

"I promise I will stay awake long enough to make certain you are delivered safely to your room."

And he promised himself that he would leave her at the door because if he did not, he would find it very difficult to leave her at all tonight.

Three

A cool breeze whipped over Kate's face as they traveled the darkened streets of St. Simone in Marc's classic convertible chick magnet. No slick, mean, manly machine had ever turned her head. She preferred comfortable sedans and comfortable shoes, which reminded her of the less-than-comfortable pumps squeezing her feet like a sadistic vise. She was tempted to kick them off but thought it best to leave on all articles of clothing, in case Marc got the wrong idea.

Like she would really try to seduce him in her current state. Her suit was wrinkled, her hair was a mess and her bra cut into her like steel fingers. Whoever invented push-up braziers should be bound at the wrists and ankles by underwire for at least forty-eight hours.

And Marc, with his suave sophistication and the wind blowing his golden hair away from his face, could easily pass as a sexy super spy like James Bond. Kate could be his girl of the month and sidekick, Roadkill. Yeah, he would definitely be interested in *that* scenario.

Marc pulled up to the curb in front of the inn and put the car in park. They were immediately joined by two other black vehicles, one in front, one in back.

Marc glanced in the rearview mirror and muttered, "For once, I wish they would leave me the hell alone."

"I'm sure they're only concerned for your safety."

"I seriously doubt any dissidents are waiting inside the hotel on the off chance that I might pay a visit in the middle of the night. They seem to forget that for most of my adult life, I've seen to my own welfare."

"But that was before you were king."

"And that seems like decades ago." He shifted in the seat to face her. "I want to thank you again, Kate."

She dislodged the rest of her wind-blown hair from her face and stared at him. "You're welcome, but I didn't really do anything."

"Don't underestimate your assistance. I'm not certain my mother would have managed the situation quite as well had you not been there."

Kate noted the weariness in his tone and in his eyes. "What do you think will happen now? With the baby, I mean."

"Right now, I'm too bloody tired to worry about it." He brushed one stubborn strand of hair away from her face. "I'm sure you're exhausted, too, although you look very beautiful at the moment."

Kate's eyes widened. "You're kidding, right?"

"No. I'm very serious."

That dog don't hunt, Kate thought, her grandfather's favorite saying. She would do well to remember that Marc DeLoria was a master of seduction, and obviously desperate if he considered her beautiful when she was sporting the results of wind-wrecked hair and an infantile food fight.

Desperate? Ha! His little black book was probably as big as her *Physicians' Desk Reference.* In fact, he'd probably utilized this very hotel for clandestine affairs.

"I've never been at this inn before," he said, as if challenging her assumption.

Kate studied the red brick building's facade and the flower boxes framing the windows to avoid his continued scrutiny. "It has old-world charm, Your Highness." Marc wasn't suffering in the charm department, either.

"Kate, as long as we're in private, you may call me Marc."

Her gaze snapped from the building to him. "What if I slip up at some point in time?"

He grinned, revealing his drop-dead gorgeous dimples. "Then it's off with your head."

Kate circled her hands around her throat. "Maybe I should just stick to Your Highness. Hard to treat patients without a head."

He looked suddenly solemn. "Seriously, I would appreciate you calling me Marc. I could use a friend."

She could use some strength. "Okay, Marc. I'll be your friend."

"Thank you."

He looked so appreciative, so sincere, so darned sexy that Kate had the strongest urge to lean over and kiss him senseless.

Party's over.

Kate needed to go upstairs, take a bath and crawl into bed. Alone. Before she did something really stupid, like convince herself that he might actually find her desirable not only as a friend, but also as a lover. How absurd. "Thanks for the ride. I can manage from here."

"Nonsense." He moved with the speed of a cougar as he slid out of the car and rounded the hood before she even had a chance to draw a breath.

Kate stared at him when he opened her door, afraid to move, to speak.

"Well?" he asked. "What are you waiting for?"

Her pulse to return to normal. "Really, I can see myself in."

His grin outshone the moon. "And disobey the king?"

"Since you put it that way, I guess I'll have to submit or risk the gallows."

Obviously she had already lost her head for letting him escort her. Only to the lobby, she reminded herself. She would say goodbye then go upstairs alone.

Marc followed Kate into the red-carpeted vestibule absent of people except for the forty-something man sitting behind the registration desk, looking totally disinterested in the king and his entourage's sudden arrival. Had Marc told her the truth, or was his appearance at the inn a common occurrence?

She was too worn out to contemplate that now. She needed sleep. When she turned to dismiss Marc, he asked, "Do you have your room key?"

She fumbled in her bag, withdrew the key and held it up. "Right here, so I'm all set. I'll see you in the morning."

He took the key from her hand, easy as pie. "I'll see you to your room."

Of all the sneaky sovereigns. Maybe she should summon a bodyguard for her own protection. Not that Marc seemed like the kind to do her bodily harm. But he could certainly do things to her body that she'd never before experienced, that much she knew. He'd been doing it all day without even touching her.

"I can make it to my room just fine." Kate tried to recover the key but before she could, he quickly tucked it into his pants pocket. She didn't dare try to go after it, since rifling in the king's pocket would probably be the ultimate breach in etiquette. Mighty fun, though.

Taking her by the elbow, Marc guided Kate up the staircase. Once they reached the room, he faced her and said, "Are you afraid of me, Kate?"

"Of course not." She was more afraid of herself and her own vulnerability where he was concerned.

"You have no need to be." He held up his hands, palms forward. "I promise my intentions are honorable."

"That's too bad." Who said that? Surely not Kate the Crusader—able to thwart all come-ons with a single put-down. But he hadn't been coming on to her at all. Maybe subconsciously she was wishing he had. What else could explain her suggestive remark?

Leaning forward, closing the space between their faces, he said, "In what way would that be bad?"

"I was just spouting off, that's all."

"That's all?" he repeated in a rough, seductive whisper.

That wasn't all, Kate thought as he came closer and closer, in slow motion it seemed, his lips only inches from hers.

She wanted this so badly. Wanted to feel his mouth on hers, wanted to know that he did see her as more than a physician, more than a friend. Know that the thought of his being her lover wasn't absurd after all.

But instead of kissing her, Marc framed her face in his palms and tipped his forehead against hers. "We can't do this, Kate."

She glanced to her right to see one bodyguard positioned at the landing, facing the descending stairs. "I understand. We have an audience."

"It's not only that. Nothing can happen between us."

Kate lowered her eyes at the same moment her heart took a dive. "I know. I'm not exactly suitable."

"You're wrong." He tipped her chin up, forcing her to look at him. "You are a beautiful, remarkable woman, Kate. And it would be incredibly easy to kiss you right now, to back you into your room, remove all your clothing and make love with you all through the night. But because of who I am, I don't have that luxury. I still have too much to prove."

"What do you have to prove?"

"That I've not bedded every woman from Belize to Great Britain."

"You haven't?"

His smile was cynical. "No. I've escorted quite a few women in my time, and I've not been a long-term celibate, but there have not been as many lovers in my life as most have assumed."

Long-term celibate? She wanted to ask him how long had it been since he'd had a lover. But it really didn't matter. He couldn't be hers. "So you're saying that you can't be involved with anyone?"

"Not at this time. Not until I can establish myself as a serious leader, and then only when I'm ready to settle into a marriage. I doubt I will be ready for that for quite some time."

Kate stepped back and wrapped her arms around her middle to mask the sudden chills. "Well, thanks for letting me know." She hated the disappointment in her tone but had to admit she liked what he had said—that he did find her desirable. That he had actually had the same thoughts she'd had all day. But that didn't change the fact that their relationship would have to remain platonic. And she might as well accept it, beginning now, even if she didn't like it.

Again he touched her face. "Kate, it is as much for your sake as it is for mine. The people of Doriana are basically kind, but they can also be judgmental when it comes to their leaders. I wouldn't want you to get hurt."

Kate could certainly accept that, but she already did hurt a little knowing that she couldn't have him, not that she'd ever really believed she could.

After checking her watch, she tried to smile. "It's really late. Have a good night. I'll see you in the morning."

He took her palm and raised it to his lips for a gentle kiss. "Sleep well, Kate."

He brushed another kiss across her cheek, then turned and walked away, leaving Kate stunned into silence, tingling at the place where his lips had been.

Kate recognized that a secret part of her still loved the man buried beneath the facade—the carefree man who existed before the kingdom had carried away his freedom.

Even if she could only be Marc's friend, nothing could stop her from attempting to lighten his spirit, ease his burden, help him have a little fun, a little adventure.

After all, that's what friends were for.

The shrill of a phone had Kate bolting upright from deep sleep. Disoriented, she thought she was back in the hospital on-call room. She fumbled for the phone and answered with the habitual Dr. Milner, as if she were still a resident.

"I'm sorry to bother you so late, Kate, but I'm having a problem with Cecile."

Cecile? The baby. She wasn't at the hospital; she was in a foreign country. The man on the other end of the line wasn't someone on staff; he was the king. A distressed-sounding king at that.

Kate sat up and glanced at the bedside clock. Almost midnight. "What's wrong?"

"I'm not certain. Beatrice and I have tried everything to calm her before she wakes my mother, but I'm afraid we're failing miserably. Could you suggest anything?"

"She's had a bottle?"

"Several. The last one landed on my forehead."

Kate fought back laughter over the image of a six-month-old using a royal forehead as target practice. "Her diaper's dry?"

"Yes. Beatrice has changed her several times. All those bottles, you know."

"And rocking her—"

"Hasn't done any good. She's determined to protest, very loudly." .

Oh, well. So much for sleep. "I'll come and see what I can do."

"Are you certain?"

"I'm sure."

"I'll send Nicholas right away."

"I'll be ready."

"And Kate, I truly appreciate this."

No problem, and it really wasn't. She'd grown accustomed to odd hours and very little sleep during medical school and residency. She'd also learned to dress quickly, which she did, in jeans, T-shirt and sneakers, sans bra. If she had to tend to a baby in the middle of the night, comfort would have to take precedence over class.

By the time she retrieved her standard black medical bag and hurried through the front door of the inn, Mr. Nicholas was waiting for her outside the limousine. He greeted her with a polite smile and, "Good evening, Dr. Milner. Quite a nice night for a drive."

Kate returned his smile. "A really nice night for sleep."

"I am sure the king will be very happy to see you," he said as he opened the back door.

Pausing with her hand on top of the car, Kate said, "He's having a tough time, huh?"

"I believe His Brilliance has been bested by a baby."

Kate chuckled at Nicholas as she climbed inside the Rolls. She'd seen true affection in the man's eyes when he'd delivered the dig at Marc's station.

They rode in silence as Nicholas wove the car along the winding roads leading to the palace. The route was illuminated by the moon, higher in the sky than it had been when she'd been with Marc earlier.

Marc.

She'd hoped to avoid him until morning. In reality, he'd been in her dreams—an odd, surreal dream where he was riding to her rescue on a massive white steed—totally naked. Such a shame that the phone had awakened her before she got to the good part. Now she really needed to get a grip.

On arrival at the palace, a very forlorn, disheveled Beatrice directed Kate to the nursery. She entered the room to find Marc wearing a gaping white dress shirt and navy pajama bottoms, sprawled out among the randomly discarded bottles and toys, his eyes closed and his head tipped back against the crib. Cecile sat in his lap, looking sassy and content as she chewed on a plastic duck, drooling like a leaky faucet.

A priceless picture. The portrait of father and daughter, and that thought gave Kate pause.

She couldn't think about that now. She had to consider the baby's well-being.

"Hey, little one," Kate said softly. "What are you doing up so late?"

"She's bent on torturing me." Marc spoke without opening his eyes, his voice gruff from frustration and probably lack of sleep.

Cecile smiled a toothless grin and squealed with glee. Totally smitten, Kate set down the bag and grabbed the baby into her arms. Only then did Marc come to his feet, giving Kate an up close and personal view of his bare chest—a really, really nice chest...

Examine the baby, Kate silently admonished. *You're here to see about the baby.*

Kate turned her attention to little Cecile, whose eyes looked clear, bright and alert. No signs of obvious illness. In fact, Cecile looked happier than she had all day.

Kate glanced at Marc over the top of the baby's head. "My

diagnosis is that little Cecile is suffering from separation anxiety."

"She's not the only one who's suffering," Marc said then moved to Kate's side to lay a gentle hand on Cecile's forehead, belying his annoyed tone. "Are you certain she doesn't have a fever?"

The parental concern in Marc's voice surprised Kate. "I take it you didn't check it."

He looked more than a little alarmed. "I would not even attempt such a delicate matter."

Kate rested her cheek against Cecile's and found it cool. "I'll take her temp but I imagine it's normal. She doesn't look at all feverish. She could be teething, though."

Marc held up his pointer. "I have no doubt about that since she has spent the past hour or so chewing my fingers until I located the duck."

Kate smiled. "If you don't mind, look in my bag and get me the thermometer."

Marc complied and held it up. "Is this it?"

"Yes. Bring it here."

He eyed the instrument with disdain. "Isn't this rather large for such a small child?"

"It's made for infants."

"I'll leave the room."

"Why? It's painless."

Marc shifted his weight from one leg to the other, looking uncomfortable. "That would be the opinion of one who did not have to suffer the indignity."

Kate realized Marc had never seen a digital thermometer before. Smiling, she slipped it in the baby's ear. After the beep sounded, she checked the reading. "Normal."

Marc's expression heralded his relief. "Now why in the devil didn't they have those when I was a boy and my mother thought that every sniff warranted a check?"

"The wonders of modern medicine." Kate glanced at the bag resting on the dressing table. "Are those her things?"

"Yes."

She strolled around the room, bouncing Cecile gently in hopes that she might become sleepy. "Look through it and see if you can find a security blanket or toy. She might need that to go to sleep."

Marc rifled through the contents and withdrew a clear plastic bag. "This is all I can find aside from her clothes."

Kate strolled to his side to examine the object—the probable answer to the sleep dilemma. A pacifier. "Take it out and wash it off with hot water, then bring it back to me."

Without a word, Marc went into the adjacent bathroom and then came out a few moments later, holding the pacifier by its pink plastic ring as if it were radioactive.

When Cecile caught sight of it, she whimpered and opened and closed her tiny fists as if to say, "Hand it over now, Buster!" Marc relinquished it to her and she popped it into her mouth, then laid her head against Kate's breast.

Kate paced the room a few moments longer as the baby's eyes grew heavy, then finally closed. Carefully she laid her in the crib, covered her with a blanket, and turned down the lamp, leaving the room in darkness except for a small nightlight near the door.

She turned to discover Marc had disappeared. Obviously he'd carted himself off to bed. Obviously she was wrong, she realized when she stepped into the corridor, closed the door and turned to find him standing there—right there—one shoulder cocked against the doorframe.

He sent her a sleepy and overtly sexy smile. "You're a genius, Kate."

She shrugged. "Not really. I used to baby-sit to earn extra money, so I've had some practice with the nighttime ritual. And pacifiers."

"Ah, so that explains why Cecile responds to you so well. Your skill with children is very apparent. You must be a remarkable doctor."

"Thank you. I think you handled the situation well. Not many men would've stayed up with a baby that wasn't theirs?" She hadn't meant to say that, much less end the sentence on a question.

"She's not mine, Kate," he said adamantly, then more gently, "but she is quite the charmer when she wants to be. She actually smiled at me a few times."

If only Kate could believe that Cecile was fathered by someone else. Hopefully they would soon learn the truth, if not through medical means, then through an investigation if the mother or father didn't come forward. And how could a mother give up such a beautiful child? Unless she didn't have the means to care for her. Marc definitely had the means.

"I do hope she stays asleep for a few hours," Marc added. "Oddly enough, I'm now quite awake."

So was Kate. Sleep was the last thing she wanted, with him staring at her expectantly.

Attempting to focus on something other than his alluring eyes, Kate's gaze dropped to the gaping shirt that revealed his naked chest, well-toned and tempting with its golden color and a patch of brown hair between his nipples. And below that she caught a glimpse of his navel and the stream of darker masculine hair leading downward, but no birthmark. Where in the heck was the birthmark? And where in the heck was her brain? This was no time to eyeball his very male anatomy. And it wasn't like she hadn't seen a naked man before. In fact, she'd seen several, but not many who looked as well developed as Marc DeLoria.

She forced her gaze up and blurted, "Thank goodness for those pacifiers."

"I find it amazing that a rubber nipple would be so appealing to a child." His grin deepened, showing off his dimples to full advantage. "As a man, I personally prefer something more natural."

Oh, no. Much too late at night for sexual innuendo. Kate pointed a finger at him. "You really are a rogue, King DeLoria."

"And that is your fault."

"My fault?"

"You bring out that side of me." He inched a little closer, seeming to steal the air from the atmosphere with the scent of soap that reminded Kate of spring, warm and wonderful. "I hope this doesn't mean you'll now refuse to be my friend." His voice was a low, deep hum—hypnotic, enticing.

Kate pretended to consider it while trying not to lose her bearings in the depths of his deep blue eyes. "I guess I'll cut you some slack this time. I'll still be your friend."

"Good. I have an idea how we can spend the rest of the evening together." He leaned forward and Kate's resolve melted completely when he murmured, "If you're interested in a little friendly late-night adventure."

Four

A midnight raid on the royal kitchen.

That was Marc DeLoria's idea of adventure—and Kate's biggest disappointment of the evening. She'd been hoping for a midnight swim in the moat, although, come to think of it, she hadn't seen a moat. At the very least, she'd been hoping for a walk in the palace gardens. She had seen those when she'd first arrived—beautifully manicured gardens with roses and topiaries and a fountain set in the middle of a reflecting pool.

But instead of taking a romantic stroll with the king, she was standing in the middle of a cavernous kitchen while Marc rummaged through a lower cabinet looking for heaven only knew what. However, he was bent over at the moment, giving Kate a really nice view of his bottom, sheathed in a thin pair of pajamas that showcased the finer points of his dignified derrière. She wondered if that was where the birthmark might be found. With just a few steps forward, and a quick tug, she could find out.

Not a good idea.

She could look all she wanted, but she couldn't touch. He'd made that quite clear outside her hotel room door. No touching allowed. No kissing. No covert rendezvous on the palace grounds, or any grounds, for that matter. But she could still fantasize about it—about him—and remember the words he had spoken earlier in a voice that had nearly brought her to her knees.

…it would be incredibly easy to kiss you right now, to back you into your room, remove all your clothing and make love with you all through the night.

It was definitely getting hot in the castle kitchen. Kate was practically going up in flames and Marc hadn't even turned on the stove.

"I've found it." Marc straightened and showed her a sauté pan along with his sexy and oh-so-charming smile.

Was he planning to make breakfast? Kate's belly roiled in protest. She didn't eat heavy meals in the middle of the night. "I'm not really fond of eggs."

"Nor am I. But I do have a fondness for crepes."

Kate leaned back against the spotless workstation centered in the room. "I know you didn't learn how to cook in the biology lab."

He set the pan on the stove and turned on the burner beneath it before facing her again. "Someone taught me how to make crepes."

Kate assumed the "someone" had been a woman. "I'm sure she got a kick out of teaching a king to cook."

"Yes, and she taught me many things."

Just as Kate had suspected. "Oh, really? Such as?"

"How to tie my shoes, how to read. Her name was Mrs. Perrine, my first nanny."

"Your nanny?"

"You thought I was referring to some nubile young woman.

I assure you Mrs. Perrine was anything but nubile or young. She was as tough as any headmaster, but she did have a way with crepes."

"I'm looking forward to sampling yours."

He sent her another killer grin. "My crepes?"

He pinned her in place with his blue eyes and suggestive tone. No touching, a little voice warned her. No nothing, just friendship. "Yes, I'm looking forward to trying your crepes, Your Highness. Or maybe I should say Your Chefness, since Mr. Nicholas isn't around."

"Marc will suffice," he said as he retreated to the monstrous refrigerator and rummaged around some more, withdrawing two covered bowls and a block of butter. He set the items on the counter next to Kate and opened the bowls. One held strawberries, the other a stack of what looked to be pancakes.

"Actually," he said, "the cook has already prepared the crepes, so I will only need to prepare the filling."

Kate crossed her arms over her middle. "Is there anything I can do to help?"

He gave her a visual once-over, pausing slightly when his gaze passed over her breasts. "You need only stand there and look beautiful, since you seem to do that very well."

Sheesh. Beautiful? She was bare-faced and bleary-eyed. "You are such a liar, Marc DeLoria."

His expression went stern. "I have never lied to you, Kate. I have no reason to lie."

Remorse brought heat of a different kind to Kate's face. Why couldn't she stop throwing around the "L" word? "I'm sorry, it's just that I'm not used to men saying those kinds of things to me."

Marc took a cutting board and knife from the counter and began slicing the strawberries, precisely, slowly. "I assure you, Kate, men have said you're beautiful, even if not to your face. Perhaps you give off signals that indicate you don't wish that kind of attention."

Kate frowned. "Do you really think…I mean…do I?"

He leveled his eyes on hers. "You do."

Kate had never considered that before, but maybe he was right. Maybe she had been too afraid to make herself that accessible for fear that she would be rejected. "Then you're saying I'm a snob?"

"No. You're friendly enough yet you still retain an aloofness, as if you are untouchable. Some men find that very intimidating."

She thought of her one medical school fling with Trevor Allen and how he'd often complained that she seemed to save all her emotions for her parents and her patients. "Do you find it intimidating?"

"No. I find it very appealing."

A network of chills slid down Kate's spine as Marc continued to look at her with eyes that could liquefy the stainless steel appliances. How many women had succumbed to his overt sexuality? Probably plenty. And she shouldn't want to be among them, but for some stupid reason, she did.

Glossing over the moment, Kate turned around and propped her elbows on the counter, her palms supporting her jaws. "Are you sure I can't help you with something? I feel so useless, just standing here looking *beautiful*."

His smile finally reappeared. "Can you melt butter?"

She was melting every time he flashed his dimples. "Yes, I can do that. How much?"

He took a large wooden spoon from a ceramic container, scooped a large chunk of butter from the block then handed it to Kate. "Put this in the pan and watch it for a moment to make sure it doesn't burn."

Kate took her place at the stove and slapped the butter into the already heated pan. It sizzled just like the blood in her veins when Marc came up behind her and added the strawberries and brown sugar, his solid arms forming a frame around her.

"Stir that, please." His warm breath caressed her neck.

"Stir it," she repeated as if the instructions might be too complex. How ridiculous was that? She'd been through med school, for heaven's sake. She could cook a few strawberries.

Marc went away for a time and she glanced at him now and then over her shoulder while he mixed whipped cream in a bowl. He returned to the stove with a ladle filled with a clear liquid. Some kind of liqueur, Kate presumed, considering the pungent aroma. Again he stood behind her as he heated the ladle over another burner for a few seconds before igniting it with a gold lighter. The flame rose from the ladle then spread over the strawberry mixture like a blue blanket as Marc poured it into the pan. The flame quietly died away, but the fire spreading through Kate when Marc's hand came to rest on her waist singed her through and through.

"Now what?" she asked, surprised she had recovered her voice.

"We wait until the alcohol burns for a while."

Marc's voice, the heat radiating from his body so close to hers, acted on Kate as if she'd consumed the entire bottle of liqueur. She leaned back against him for support and his arms came around her, strong and inviting. Then he slowly turned her around in those solid arms until she was facing him.

Again Kate witnessed the indecision warring in his eyes, but this time she also saw desire win out before he cradled her jaw in his palms, then touched his mouth to hers. Yet he only brushed her lips with tempered, chaste kisses, drawing back each time until she thought she might go crazy. She wasn't sure if it was uncertainty on Marc's part or if he was waiting for her to make the next move. The need to know how it would feel to have him kiss her completely drove Kate to clasp his nape and pull his mouth full against hers to finally have what she craved.

Although she had imagined Marc's kiss, although she'd

thought she was ready, Kate soon realized she'd been totally deceiving herself. Skill wasn't an adequate enough word to describe Marc DeLoria's expertise. Never before had she been kissed so softly yet so thoroughly. He used his tongue like a feather, invading her mouth with fine strokes without being at all intrusive. And Kate felt it down to her knees and lower.

He pulled her against him and slid his hand down her back to her hips. She realized the result of this spontaneous kiss when Marc pressed against her, showing Kate up front that he was very affected. And so was she.

After abruptly breaking the kiss, Marc took a step back, rubbed a hand over his jaw and exhaled a long breath. "My apologies, Kate. Something about you standing at the stove made me forget myself."

Kate wasn't sure whether to be flattered or insulted. She was, however, very winded and very warm. "Oh, so do you have one of those French maid fantasies or do you just prefer the domestic type?"

His expression turned serious. "I have to remember that nothing has changed since I left you at your hotel door. We really can't be doing this."

"We just did."

"I know, and it shouldn't happen again."

Kate couldn't stop her smile when she realized he sounded as if he were trying to convince himself it *wouldn't* happen again. "Then I guess we should avoid kitchens if seeing a woman standing at the stove turns you on."

He smiled reluctantly. "You're probably right, and I believe the strawberries are done now."

Obviously, so were they, Kate decided.

Marc assembled the crepes and placed them on plates while Kate looked on, still reeling from the kiss. She had to hand it to Marc, he had an iron will. Or maybe he was just being nice to her. But she hadn't seen *nice* in his expression when she'd been in his arms. She'd seen want, maybe even need. And her thoughts at that moment wouldn't qualify as nice, either. But from this point forward, she would probably have to settle for just that single memory.

They carried the dessert into a comfortable den with a cushy tweed couch and a fireplace in the corner. Marc set his plate on the coffee table in front of the sofa and settled beside Kate.

Kate waited for him to take the first bite, but instead he cut into one of her crepes and held it to her lips. "Your first sample."

She slid the crepe into her mouth and savored the flavors of strawberries, whipped cream and sugar; the delicate crepe practically dissolved in her mouth. "This is almost sinful."

His eyes held fast to hers. "That would depend on your definition of sin."

"Calories," she added after she swallowed another bite. "And carbs, especially when they take up residence on your thighs."

His gaze drifted to her thighs, then traveled slowly back up again to her face. "I doubt that you need to worry about that."

"From your mouth to my metabolism's ear."

"I hope you'll put away all your concerns and simply enjoy."

Kate did as Marc asked and ate every last bite of the crepes, all the while wondering if Marc's comment about sinful behavior went beyond indulging in dessert. But she didn't dare hope, didn't dare consider anything more than spending time with him as a friend.

After they both finished, Marc grabbed the remote control and snapped on the television positioned in the entertainment center. He flipped through the channels, pausing at one nature program heralding the mating habits of the mongoose. With a groan, he changed the channel to a French-speaking movie where two people seemed engaged in a battle of wills.

After tossing the remote back on the table, he leaned back

against the couch. "Not much variety this time of the night, so I suppose we'll have to settle for this. Unless you're ready for bed."

Kate assumed he'd meant alone and right now that didn't float her boat. "Funny, I'm not all that tired, although I probably should be."

"Then perhaps this movie will put you to sleep."

"It could, since I have no idea what they're saying."

Marc draped his arm over the back of the sofa, only a few inches separating their bodies. "The man's name is Jean-Michel and he's telling the woman, Genevieve, that he must leave her since he belongs to another."

"The cad. What did she say to that?"

"She says *Tu me veux. Je te défie de me dire que je me suis trompée.* She claims he wants her and she's daring him to deny it."

Hearing Marc speaking in French in a low, husky voice blanketed Kate in chills. She glanced at him and realized he'd moved much closer, rekindling the fire that had been smoldering deep within her all evening. "Is he denying it?"

Marc's gaze drifted to her mouth. "*C'est impossible.* It's impossible for him to deny that he wants her."

The conviction in Marc's voice, the heat in his eyes, fed Kate's optimism that he was speaking of his own desire—desire for her. Or maybe she simply wanted him so badly that she'd invented something that wasn't really there.

Turning her attention away from Marc and back to the movie, she got the full effect of Jean-Michel's weakness for Genevieve. Now tangled together in a passionate embrace, the lovers' actions spoke loud and clear in that age-old universal language of love. Kate twitched when the camera panned in for an up close and very personal shot of the actors' lips melded together, their hands roving over each other as if they couldn't quite touch enough to be satisfied. She squirmed some more when the couple tore at each other's clothing until they were completely, unabashedly naked.

"This must be a cable channel," she muttered, all too aware of how dumb and unsophisticated that must have sounded.

"Actually, no. Freedom of expression is highly regarded here. Nudity is considered natural and beautiful. So is lovemaking."

Kate's heart bounded into her throat when Marc's arm came to rest on her shoulder, his fingertips tracing slow, random circles on her upper arm as if drawing his name in the sand. Marking his territory so to speak, and making Kate mindful of how much the movie and his touch were affecting her.

"Maybe we should watch something else," she said.

Marc nuzzled his face in her hair, taking her by surprise and her senses by storm. "Does it make you uncomfortable?"

Kate bit her bottom lip, hard. "A little."

"In what way?"

"I don't know." She did know, and Marc probably knew, too. The uncensored sex on the screen, Marc's close proximity, was turning her on, turning her into a woman on the verge of asking him at the very least to kiss her again.

She didn't have to ask, and this time there was no reluctance in Marc's kiss, no hesitation. So focused was Kate on the welcome invasion of his tongue, the soft insistence of his lips, that she was only mildly aware of the lovers' soft moans coming from the TV, Marc's evening whiskers abrading her chin and his hand traveling up and down her side, grazing her breast with each pass.

Time seemed suspended and Kate acknowledged she could go on kissing him forever. But a girl could only be kissed this way for so long without other parts of her body becoming present and accounted for. Her nipples hardened against his chest. Fire spread through her belly and settled between her thighs in a dull throb.

As if some wild wanton creature had crawled beneath her

skin, Kate lifted her leg over Marc's thighs. He groaned against her mouth and took her down onto the couch, where he settled on top of her, his own leg dividing her legs. He momentarily broke the kiss to raise her shirt, untie his robe and push it open, before taking her mouth once more. But he didn't use his hand to tantalize her; he used his chest, lightly rubbing her bare breasts, drawing away slightly then rubbing again and again, in maddening circular motions. The fine veneer of chest hair tickled her nipples into hard, sensitive buds and sent a wash of dampness between her thighs.

Unraveled by his skill, his welcome weight and deep kisses, Kate tilted her hips up to feel him more, as if that might soothe the ache. And she did feel him, every solid inch of him, through the thin material of his pajamas.

As if he recognized her need, Marc slid his hand between them at her abdomen. The tug on the snap of her jeans only heightened Kate's excitement and spurred her anticipation.

Then suddenly, there was nothing. No kisses. No touches. No Marc.

Kate opened her eyes and looked up to find Marc standing several feet away, his back to her, both hands laced together behind his neck. And then came Kate's complete mortification in a few moments of silence that seemed to last hours.

"I'm sorry, Kate."

He was apologizing again, and Kate was without a doubt more embarrassed than she'd ever been her entire life. She pulled her shirt down, scooted to the edge of the sofa and clutched her disheveled hair by the roots. "I can't imagine what you must think of me right now."

He sat beside her, his expression remorseful as he took her hand into his. "Would you like to know what I think of you? I think you're the most incredible, sensual woman I've encountered in many years, if not ever. I think that if I hadn't remembered why we cannot do this, I would be inside of you at this moment and that would be wrong."

His words gave her a courage she'd never known before, at least where men were concerned. "Why would it be wrong, Marc? We're both adults. No one's around. No one would have to know."

He released a harsh sigh. "Because I could only offer you a casual affair, in secret. Because you're a good woman, Kate, and you deserve to be treated as such, not hidden away from the world."

Kate had always been the good girl. The good, reliable girl. She'd grown tired of bearing that label, weary of being that girl. Besides, she was a woman now, with a woman's desires and needs—and she was with a man who had the knowledge and the means to take her beyond the limit. But he wasn't willing to answer those needs, at least not now.

Kate wrenched her hand from his and crossed her arms over her chest thinking that might alleviate the sudden cold that had replaced the heat, a futile gesture. "I guess you're right, Marc. So let's just chalk up my total lack of restraint to my current state of jet lag. I should probably go back to the hotel now."

When Kate stood, Marc caught her wrist. "Stay here, tonight, Kate. With me. You need your rest. We can both sleep on the sofa."

"I'm not sure that's a good idea," Kate said, although regardless of her reckless behavior and his subsequent rejection, she would like nothing more than to wake in Marc's arms.

After gathering a throw from the opposite arm of the couch, Marc tied his robe, worked his way to the corner of the sofa and pulled her down into his arms. "Stretch out your legs and put your head on my chest. I promise to keep my hands to myself."

"Darn it."

He tossed the throw over them both. "Don't make this any

harder than it already is, fair lady, or I'm afraid I'll have to lock you in the dungeon."

Kate felt giddy and punch-drunk. "Exactly how hard is it?"

Marc cracked a crooked smile. "You could not begin to imagine."

Oh, but she didn't have to rely on her imagination. She'd gotten the extent of "it" a few moments before and in the kitchen. She doubted she would ever forget how he'd felt against her. But right now she should try to sleep. Morning would come all too soon, and her time alone with Marc would probably come to an end. After tonight, she had no doubt he would probably avoid her from here on out. And maybe that was best. After all, he was a king, she was a doctor, and he had something to prove—that he could resist her. That made Kate smile as she closed her eyes.

Imagine that. King Marcel DeLoria had found her irresistible.

"Marcel, wake up."

Marc forced his eyes open to find his mother standing before the sofa, Cecile propped on one hip, flailing her tiny arms about as if directing an orchestra. What in the devil was Mary doing up this time of the night and why was she fully dressed as if ready to hold court? Unless it was already morning. Surely not. No more than an hour had passed since he'd finally drifted off, or at least it seemed that way.

Every molecule of his body ached from the position he'd kept for the past few hours, one part in particular, thanks to the woman in his arms. Some time during the night, Kate had inadvertently landed her palm on his groin—and for some insane reason, he'd left it there. Luckily the throw and his robe covered his lower body, adequately concealing his predicament from his matriarch.

When Cecile squealed, Kate snapped up like a bedspring, tossed the cover aside and pushed her hair away from her face. "What time is it?"

Marc slid the throw back into his lap as nonchalantly as possible. "Very early," he said, his voice rough from lack of sleep, unanswered need and an abundance of annoyance.

Mary took a seat in the chair across from the sofa, Cecile in her lap happy as a lark. "It's not quite dawn. When Cecile awakened, I relieved Beatrice so she could have some sleep, since it seems our little one has her days and nights confused."

"At least someone's sleeping," Marc grumbled yet he couldn't help but smile at Cecile as she gummed his mother's favorite string of pearls hanging from Mary's throat. Only an innocent could get away with such anarchy.

When Mary surveyed Kate's disheveled appearance, Marc could almost hear the cogs turning in her mind. "I hadn't realized Kate had not returned to the hotel," she said.

Kate averted her eyes and tugged at her wrinkled T-shirt. "Actually, I did return to the hotel. Marc called and asked me to come and check on Cecile when she wouldn't sleep. He thought she was ill."

"She certainly seems well enough to me," Mary said as she brushed a kiss across the baby's cheek. Then she leveled her gaze on Marc. "I hope you didn't take advantage of Kate's courtesy, Marcel."

He glanced at Kate who was sporting a deep blush. "Mother, I assure you I did not take advantage of Kate. And if you're intimating that something sordid went on last night, you are wrong." Not that he hadn't considered it. "We were both very tired and we fell asleep during a movie."

"Of course I would not think such a thing, dear boy. Kate would never do something sordid."

He experienced a sudden surge of anger that effectively repressed any lingering effects of his desire for the doctor. "But I would?"

"I suppose not, since you appear to have on your robe, although it's difficult to tell with you clutching that throw as if you feared it might walk away."

Marc yanked the blanket aside. "Happy now, Mother? I have done nothing to compromise Kate's or my reputation." And not because he didn't want Kate; he did. Even now with her curled up on the couch, both her clothes and hair a mess, he still wanted her. Badly.

Mary sighed. "But you did leave quite a disaster in the kitchen. Cook is already grousing this morning."

"I'm afraid that's my fault," Kate said. "I meant to clean up before I fell asleep, since Marc did the cooking."

Mary sent Kate a kind look. "Nonsense, my dear. You are our guest. Marc could have cleaned up after himself, although I'm not certain he's learned the fine art of housekeeping."

His mother was obviously determined to ruin his day. "Don't you think I already have enough responsibilities, Mother?"

"Yes, dear, you do." She sent a pointed look at Cecile, causing Marc to grit his teeth.

After coming to her feet, Kate walked to the chair and said, "May I hold her?"

"Why, of course." Mary stood and relinquished Cecile to Kate.

Kate hugged the baby and kissed her cheek. "I hope you've gotten plenty of sleep, little one, since we have a busy morning ahead of us at the clinic."

Marc leaned his head against the sofa, all the energy seeming to drain from him at that moment. "I bloody well forgot about the damn test."

"Take care with your language, Marcel," Mary scolded. "You have two ladies present and one grandmother who will not tolerate disrespect."

"My apologies," Marc muttered, a long list of descriptive curses threatening to explode from his mouth. The queen mother was already laying claim to Cecile before proof of that fact existed.

"How is your headache, Mary?" Kate asked, looking uncomfortable over the exchange between mother and son.

Mary laid a hand on Kate's arm. "My dear, it is completely gone, thanks to you. That neck massage you gave me did the trick."

"It was no problem at all." She regarded Marc over her shoulder. "I learned some massage therapy while I was in med school. Pressure points, that sort of thing, to relieve tension."

Marc had a point of pressure he would greatly like Kate to relieve. Instead, his mother had received a massage and he'd only acquired a painful kink in his neck and a prominent swelling beneath his pajamas.

Kate handed the baby back to Mary and said, "Well, I guess I need to return to the hotel and freshen up before we go to the clinic."

"You must stay for breakfast, dear. Cook has begun the preparations."

Kate turned to Marc as if seeking reinforcement. "It might be better if I leave now. We need to get everything done before the clinic opens."

Marc stood. "I'll have Mr. Nicholas take you back to the hotel immediately."

"That's fine," Kate said, a hint of disappointment in her tone.

Marc had done nothing but disappoint her the past few hours; that much he knew. Last night, she had needed something from him, something he hadn't been able to give to her—and not because he hadn't wanted to. But if he'd touched her in the way that he'd wanted, he might not have been able to stop with only a touch. And if not careful, it would happen again…and again.

An hour later, Kate and Marc slipped through the clinic's back door with the baby in tow, fortunately finding the place totally deserted. In a small room at the far end of the corridor, Kate thoroughly examined Cecile, who remained content by chewing on the hem of her discarded cornflower blue dress while Marc looked on. Cecile seemed very healthy, only slightly below average in weight and height for a child of seven months, if, in fact, that was her age. Kate could only estimate unless the mother came forward. At least today they might learn more about the father, namely if he could possibly be Marc or Philippe.

With that thought, Kate took a lancet in hand to draw Cecile's blood. She hated this part the most—sticking an unsuspecting baby.

After returning to the table, she told Marc, "If you could just hold her a little, that would be a big help."

Marc frowned. "Will it hurt her very much?"

Kate smiled at the concern in his tone and expression. "Only a little finger prick, but she's not going to like it. That's why I need to make sure she doesn't move away."

Marc did as he was told, speaking to Cecile in a soothing tone while Kate applied the stick. Cecile looked surprised at first, then her tiny bottom lip quivered and she let out a wail when Kate began to knead her finger.

"That's it, sweetie," Kate said after she had enough of a sample on the glass slide. "All done here. I hope you don't hate me now."

Cecile buried her face against Marc's chest and released a few sniffles before turning back to Kate and holding out her arms.

"Obviously she doesn't hate you at all," Marc said as Kate took the baby.

Kate wondered if Marc hated her after their interlude last night. Maybe hate was too strong a word, but she doubted he was pleased by her behavior. She couldn't worry about that now. She had too much to do.

Kate swiped the downy blond hair away from Cecile's

forehead and planted a kiss there. "She's a very brave girl. Now I'll just get her dressed and you can take her home while I work on the test. Hopefully she'll be ready for a nap."

"I am most definitely ready for a nap," Marc said, his off-kilter smile reappearing. "I'm sure you are as well. We could crawl up on the sofa and see what we can find in the way of daytime programming."

Okay, so maybe she'd been wrong. Maybe he wasn't all that concerned about what had and hadn't happened last night. But it would be best for all concerned if they steered clear of that kind of situation from this point forward.

She sent him a cautioning glance. "I think we should avoid the TV at all costs."

He looked frustrated. "You're probably right. While you're dressing Cecile, I'm going to see if Dr. Martine has arrived yet. He's supposed to be on his way. I'll be back as soon as possible since it's getting late. Perhaps we'll be able to leave undetected."

"I'll see you in a while then."

Marc leaned over to kiss Cecile's cheek and for the briefest of moments, Kate thought he might kiss her, too. Instead, he turned away and quickly headed out the door.

Kate rummaged through the bag and withdrew a clean diaper to change Cecile, who wasn't altogether cooperative. Several times, Kate feared that the little girl might hurl herself off the table before Kate had the diaper secured. After success finally came, Kate pulled her up and began to dress her.

"I wish I had your energy, little one," she told her when Cecile immediately discarded the sock that Kate had just slipped on her foot. "I just know you're going to give Beatrice a run for her money today. That is, if I can get you to keep your clothes on." With effort, she finally managed to secure the rest of the buttons on Cecile's dress. "But I can't really blame you. Right now, I'd really like to get out of these slacks and shoes and take a long, hot bath."

"Do you need any assistance?"

The hairs on Kate's neck stood at attention when recognition dawned. She glanced over her shoulder to confirm her fears and found Renault leaning in the doorway with all the cockiness of a twenty-year-old jock—and only half the height and body. His sparse blond hair was slicked back, his beady brown eyes focused on the baby. So much for a quick getaway.

Kate lifted Cecile into her arms and faced the jerk, trying to affect calm when her mind was struggling to come up with an explanation. "Good morning, Dr. Renault. I wasn't expecting you so early."

"Nor I you." He moved closer and surveyed Cecile. "I've been told you would not assume your duties until tomorrow."

Evasion was probably her best line of defense, Kate decided. "That's correct."

"Yet you're examining this child."

"Yes."

"I did not see anyone in the waiting room. Does she have parents?"

"Of course she has parents. Didn't they teach you in medical school that those old folktales about storks and cabbage patches aren't true?"

Renault's smile was cynical. "I assure you, Dr. Milner, I know all the workings of procreation. You have still not answered my question. To whom does this child belong?"

Think quick, Kate. "Actually, she belongs to me."

Renault raised one bushy eyebrow. "Martine did not mention you have a child."

"Well, I do, and this is her. Cecile."

He stroked his pointy chin. "Ah, Cecile. A very fine French name. Is your husband French?"

"I don't have a husband." And that wasn't a lie.

"The baby's father, then?"

"He's not in the picture." An understatement in the first order.

Renault gave Kate a slimy visual once-over, fitting for a human slug. "I must say, you are in very fine shape given the age of this child. I admire you for that. In fact, I admire everything about you."

Kate resisted telling him where to stuff his admiration. "Thank you." She had to get away before he asked more questions. "I really need to get her home for her morning nap. But first, I have a few tests I need to run."

"Is she ill?"

"No. Just routine labs."

"I would be more than happy to assist you."

"I believe Dr. Milner is quite capable of working alone, Renault."

Kate turned to see Marc sporting a look that could wither the overhead light.

Renault didn't look the least bit concerned over Marc's presence or his sharp tone. "I am most certain, Your Highness, Dr. Milner is quite capable in all that she endeavors. I was simply trying to be accommodating."

Marc balled his hands into fists at his sides. "She doesn't need your assistance, I assure you."

Renault turned back to Kate, bowed slightly and kissed Cecile's hand. "You are a lovely girl, Cecile."

Kate wanted to cheer when Cecile pulled her hand away and hid her face against Kate's shoulder. Either she had stranger phobia or good instincts. Kate assumed the latter, considering she had taken to Kate, Marc and his mother without hesitation.

Before Renault passed Marc at the door, Marc told him, "You will practice the utmost in decorum where Dr. Milner is concerned or you will answer to me. Is that clear?"

Renault sent Kate a lecherous glance, then glared at Marc. "Quite clear, Your Majesty. I do not intend to tread on another man's territory."

With that, he was gone and Marc looked as if he could blow

a fuse when he faced Kate again. "Did he do anything inappropriate?" he demanded.

Kate considered telling him about Renault's intimations but decided to wait until later when she was assured they were alone. "His kind are a dime a dozen and I know how to handle them."

"And you will tell me if he is the least bit out of line." It wasn't a request.

"I promise I'll tell you if I have to hurt him." She handed Marc the baby and smiled. "Now you go with your…king, Cecile, and I'll be back later today." She kissed the baby's cheek one last time and reined in her urge to do the same to Marc. "Be a good girl, sweetie. I'll be back as soon as I can."

"I'm certain she'll look forward to your return." Marc leaned toward Kate's ear and whispered, "And so will I, so hurry."

Then Marc left the room, leaving Kate standing alone in a state of confusion. Couldn't Marc make up his mind? He was making her head spin with his no-we-can't and yes-we-will attitude. He did want her; that was becoming apparent to Kate each time they were together. Yet he kept saying he couldn't have her. But if Marc's resistance completely waned, how far would she allow things to go, since she recognized it wouldn't be more than a fling? Did she dare make love with him?

Yes. No question about it. She wasn't looking for a knight's rescue, only a night of incredible lovemaking. A little adventure. She wanted to experience true freedom in his arms without worrying about pleasing anyone aside from herself—and Marc DeLoria.

She shivered thinking about it, thinking about him, thinking about all the ways he could take her places she'd never been before.

Imagine that, making love with a king. Now if only the king would cooperate.

Five

After Kate conducted the lab tests, Dr. Martine asked if she could possibly see some patients—minor cases, most involving common colds and well-baby checks. She agreed and was accompanied by a very nice Australian-born nurse named Caroline, who aided Kate in interpreting conditions of those who spoke only French or Castilian, and there were more than a few.

By that afternoon, Kate was high on adrenaline but still concerned about the language barriers. She made a mental note to get out the tapes and books to study when she had a spare minute. If she ever had a spare minute. She also needed to call home soon. She hadn't spoken with her mother, hadn't even told her that she'd accepted the position. Kate refused to perceive that as a problem. It was high time for her family to learn to live without her constant attention.

Fortunately, Renault had been scarce during the day, which was probably the reason why the clinic had been running so far behind, not that Kate had minded his absence or treating his patients. She'd welcomed rejoining the world of medicine—and avoiding confronting Marc with the knowledge she now held—the test results.

After arriving back at the palace, she waited in Marc's private study with that knowledge while Mr. Nicholas summoned the king. It could be a while, Nicholas had told her, since Marc had gone out for a drive. Kate assumed this was Marc's only means to relax—or to escape. And when he found out that Cecile shared his rare blood type, he might climb back into his coveted car and keep driving.

Kate milled around the office, pulling various books from the shelves, mainly from nervousness instead of real interest. Most involved business acumen, as far as she could tell, since all were written in French. Except for one well-worn English volume of *Hamlet* that looked as though it had been handed down through the generations. Ironic, Kate decided, since to be or not to be was definitely the question of the moment in terms of Marc's possible parental ties to Cecile.

Yet he'd been so adamant he wasn't Cecile's father that Kate almost believed him. In some ways she still did, since she really had no reason not to take him at his word. She also knew that accidents happened, and unless Cecile's mother came forward, they might never know the truth.

When the phone shrilled, Kate nearly jumped out of her functional black shoes. She waited while the phone rang again for someone to answer. Maybe she should answer it. It could be Marc's private line and he might be calling her to say he'd been detained. If not, she would have to take a message.

But how should she answer? The DeLoria Residence? The King's Office?

On the fourth ring, Kate leaned over the desk, grabbed the receiver and settled for a simple, "Hello."

A long silence ensued until a breathy feminine voice asked, "Is this Marc's secretary?"

Kate was overcome with an insane spark of jealousy. "No, this is not Marc's secretary."

The woman released a grating laugh. "Then you must be my replacement. I do hope you are taking advantage of Marc's expertise. He is quite a skilled lover, isn't he? Has he taken you to the little mountain cabin yet?"

Kate had no desire to confirm or deny anything to this woman, especially since she appeared to be one of Marc's erstwhile lovers. "May I ask who's calling?"

"Why, darling, this is Elsa," she fairly purred.

As if that should mean something to Kate. "Well, Elsa, is there something I can do for you?" *Darling*.

"I am calling to see if Marc received the gift I had delivered to the palace."

Gift? Surely she didn't mean… "Does this gift happen to have blue eyes and blond hair?"

"Why yes, darling, it does. A little reminder of our time together. Tell Marc to enjoy."

The line went dead and Kate could only stare at the receiver before slamming the phone back on its cradle.

Obviously she had been wrong to believe Marc. Obviously this Elsa was Cecile's mother, if you could actually call her that. What kind of woman would just drop her baby off at a gate and then leave? A heartless, cruel woman who didn't have a maternal bone in her body.

Kate's heart felt weighted with the knowledge that her questions had now been answered. Marc had fathered a child by some flighty femme fatale who had no business being a parent. And Kate dared Marc to deny his daughter now.

Marc couldn't deny he was in a huge hurry to see Kate. He entered the palace through the back access at a fast clip, Nicholas dogging his every step. "Where is Dr. Milner now?"

"She is waiting in your study, Your Eagerness."

Marc muttered an oath. "This is no time to joke, Nicholas. Did she seem concerned about anything?"

"Actually, she did seem a bit on edge."

Striding down the corridor toward his office, Marc pulled his sunshades off his eyes and tossed them and his keys to Nicholas. "Have someone park the car, and make sure I am not disturbed until I say otherwise. Is that clear?"

Nicholas stopped outside the study and saluted. "I live to serve you."

After sending Nicholas a harsh look—which the man did not seem to heed—Marc opened his office door to find Kate leaning back against his desk, her arms stiff at her sides and her eyes reflecting displeasure. Obviously Renault had used his torrid tactics to try to bed her, or she had confirmed Cecile's blood type as his match and still believed he wasn't being truthful.

After closing the door behind him and tripping the lock, Marc decided to begin with his concerns over her colleague. "Did Renault do something to you?"

"I didn't see him again after your left. I did see a few patients after I typed Cecile's blood."

"Then you have the results?"

"Yes, and I also have a message for you." Her tone was clipped and cool, devoid of welcome.

"A message?"

"From Elsa, *darling*. She called a few minutes ago. I answered the phone because I thought it might be you."

Why in the devil was Elsa calling him? He'd made it quite clear that he wanted no contact from her, not that his demands had ever stopped her. "What did she want?"

Kate strolled around the room for a moment before facing him again. "She wanted to know if you received her gift, the one with blue eyes and blond hair. She had it delivered to the palace. So I suppose you could say the mystery of Cecile's mother is solved."

At first Marc was perplexed, until he realized what Elsa had been referring to. He couldn't stop the chuckle, not a good thing to do considering the acid look Kate sent him. If her eyes were dueling pistols, he'd be a dead man.

Marc pushed away from the door, crossed the room and reached behind the armoire to retrieve the "gift" in hopes of clearing up this whole misunderstanding.

Grabbing the edge of the frame, he withdrew the photograph and presented it to Kate. "This is Elsa's gift. An eleven-by-fourteen glossy from her recent photo shoot. You will note that she has blond hair and blue eyes." And practically no clothes on aside from a skimpy swimsuit.

Kate took the picture from him and stared at it for a time before bringing her gaze back to Marc. "She considers this a gift?"

"Elsa considers herself a gift to all mankind." He took the photo back and hid it away again behind the armoire before returning to Kate, maintaining some distance even though he wanted to kiss away her doubts. "She thought I would be interested enough to keep it as a reminder of our brief association. She was mistaken. I've meant to have Nicholas discard it, but I've not had the time with everything that's been happening of late."

"But you don't deny you were lovers."

"No, I cannot deny that." He also couldn't deny the jealousy in Kate's tone, nor could he deny that on some level that pleased him.

She narrowed her eyes. "And there's no way she could be Cecile's mother?"

"There is as much chance of Elsa being a mother as there is a chance that her breasts are real."

A hint of a smile teased at Kate's full lips, but it didn't quite form. "How can you be so sure?"

He offered his own smile, hoping to lighten the mood. "I happen to know when a woman has natural attributes."

She frowned. "I meant about her not being Cecile's mother."

So much for his attempt at humor. "If Elsa had been pregnant, she would not have abandoned the baby. That much I know."

"Then she's not just another pretty ego?"

"Elsa is very self-absorbed and she would not risk an end to her modeling career with an unplanned pregnancy. She made it quite clear she never wanted any children. And if by some chance she'd chosen to have a baby, she would have turned it into a publicity campaign, especially if that baby were mine."

Kate remained silent for a few moments as if attempting to digest the information. "Okay, I guess I believe you."

She might as well have slapped him. "You guess? Have I not given you enough proof?"

"You've provided proof that Elsa probably isn't Cecile's mother. But I have the proof that odds are Cecile is either yours or Philippe's child."

As he'd suspected. "Then she has our blood type."

"Yes. I confirmed the results with Dr. Martine."

He saw mistrust in Kate's eyes, and he hated that. "You must believe me when I tell you that Elsa was the last woman in my life for well over a year, and I have exercised the greatest care. The baby is not mine."

"It doesn't really matter what I believe."

"It does to me."

"Why?"

A difficult question, and one he had avoided asking himself. "Because you're a very special person, Kate. I need you to trust me. I know that you hold the truth in very high esteem."

Kate's gaze faltered. "I'm not beyond telling a lie, Marc. In fact, I told one today. A big one."

"You've lied to me?"

"Not you. Renault. When he came into the exam room, he started asking questions. I told him Cecile is my daughter."

He could not have asked for a better plan. "That's brilliant, Kate."

"It is?"

"Yes. Perhaps now there won't be any speculation in terms of Cecile's parentage until someone comes forward with the truth."

"*If* someone comes forward."

Marc did not foresee that happening, at least not soon. It would be up to him to clear his name. "I doubt that will be the case, but it's still imperative that we find out who the mother is. Chances are, my perfect brother was not so perfect after all."

She sent him a severe look. "Are you doing this for Cecile or for yourself? Do you want to prove that Philippe wasn't as innocent as he seemed? And if you do that, how will it affect your family?"

Kate's honesty threw Marc mentally off balance. He hadn't considered how the truth might affect his mother if they proved Philippe was Cecile's father. "I need to put this issue to bed once and for all, for everyone's sake. How I'll handle the rest remains to be seen. First, I must attempt to find out the mother's identity."

"And how do you propose to do that?"

He had no right to ask, but Kate was his only hope. "With your help."

"My help?"

"I'm only asking that you keep your ears open for any gossip. Perhaps search the hospital's records for any mysterious woman who gave birth six to eight months ago. The staff in the palace might be forthcoming with information about my brother since you're—"

"A commoner."

"Yes, in a manner of speaking."

"Then you're asking me to do a little investigating in my spare time."

"Only if you feel comfortable in doing so."

"As long as we've absolutely ruled out your lover."

He took a step forward. "*Former* lover. It's over between us, Kate."

She slowly ran a fingertip along the edge of the desk, fueling Marc's all-consuming desire for her. "Obviously you still have something she wants."

"She wants attention and not necessarily only from me."

Kate leaned back against the desk, using her arms as a brace, thrusting her breasts forward, driving Marc to distraction. "Are you sure about that? She's very vocal about your skills as a lover. So are you, Marc?"

A fool? A man too weak to resist her charms? "Am I what?"

"A skilled lover?"

Marc was only certain about one thing—he couldn't ignore Kate's query, asked in a sensual voice that threatened his control. Couldn't ignore her simple black slacks and plain white blouse that would be easy to remove. Couldn't ignore the tightness in his groin when she streaked her tongue over her lower lip.

"I do not make it a habit to speculate on my skill," he said, clinging to his last strand of restraint.

"Maybe I should judge for myself."

"You have no idea what you're asking, Kate." He did know all too well she recognized the power she had over him at that moment, and he found that incredibly hard to resist.

She swept her dark hair away from her face with one hand. "You're wrong, Marc. I know exactly what I'm asking, and so do you. Does your expertise live up to the hype? Are you a good lover?"

"Good is an interesting term. Good only comes when you do not aspire to be great."

"Do you aspire to be a great lover, Marc DeLoria?"

"I refuse to settle for mediocrity in any of my endeavors."

She challenged him with a look, dared him with a sultry smile, enticed him with words when she said, "Then prove it."

Marc was losing his tenuous hold on his common sense. He only knew that if he didn't get away from Kate now, he would kiss her—deeply and without reservation. Touch her without hesitation. Without consideration of the consequences. He had no call to want her as much as he did. He had too much to consider in light of his position and too little to offer her beyond mutual pleasure. But he did want her, and he'd be damned if he had her—or damned if he didn't.

Propelled by his weakness for this woman, Marc closed the distance between them in two strides and braced his palms on the desk on either side of her. He sought her mouth in a rush, as if he couldn't survive without exploring the territory once more. She opened to him, played her tongue against his, pushed him to a point where he could easily dispense with all formality and clothing to get inside her immediately. But he rejected that notion. If he could touch her, taste her, tempt her, then that would be enough. It would have to be enough.

After breaking the kiss, he settled his face in the hollow below her throat, pressing his lips there while inhaling her enticing fragrance.

"Marc, I thought you said we couldn't." Her voice was a teasing, breathy caress at his ear.

"Shouldn't," he murmured then slid his tongue down the cleft between her breasts, stopping where the opening of her blouse ended and buttons began, knowing he should not go any farther. But knowing what he shouldn't do did nothing to quell the urge to do what he wanted to do. To her, with her.

Kate threaded her hands through his hair, back and forth in long, torturous strokes. "Maybe we should go somewhere more private."

He straightened and slipped the first button on her blouse, ignoring the persistent voice telling him to stop. "I've locked the door." He released two more buttons, keeping his gaze fixed on Kate's eyes, searching for any sign of protest. He saw nothing but need. "I gave orders that we are not to be disturbed."

"Very resourceful," she said, followed by a shaky smile that indicated nervousness, but not reluctance.

Finally, Marc parted her blouse, exposing her bra, which he unhooked with a quick flip of one finger beneath the front closure before pushing it aside with both hands. His gaze roved over her breasts, round and pink tinged to match the flush on her face when he lifted her up and scated her on the desk's edge.

As he traced a path around one rosy tip with his finger, Kate watched his movements, her chest rising and falling in rapid succession. *"Tu es parfaite,"* he whispered. " Perfect."

Dipping his head, he drew one nipple into his mouth, relishing the feel of her against his tongue. He wanted more. He wanted it all. He wanted to undo her slacks, slip his hand inside, experience her wet heat. He wanted to open his own fly, give himself some blessed relief, and thrust inside her.

When Kate released a soft, sexual sound, reality forced its way into his psyche and he took a step back. "We have to stop this, Kate."

"Why?"

Marc had so many reasons, but he began with the most important. "I have nothing to protect you against pregnancy, and God knows I do not need another complication."

Kate's face fell as if it had the weight of the world attached. "Complication? So that's what I am to you?"

"No…that's not…" What in the hell could he say? Yes, she was a complication. His overwhelming desire was very complicated, as were his feelings for her that he did not dare examine. "Look, Kate, I've done what I said I would not do. I've proven my weakness for you against my better judgment."

"Weakness for me, or for women in general?"

That brought seething anger to the surface of Marc's attempts at a calm facade. "I've spent almost a year being celibate, and it was not due to a lack of propositions. I've met many women over that time, in many different places, and not one has tempted me the way that you do. Only you, Kate, and no one else."

She looked a bit more relaxed, if not totally pleased, as she redid her bra. "And what do you propose we do now? Ignore our attraction to each other?" She paused with a hand on the blouse and looked at him thoughtfully. "Or were you just trying to prove a point?"

"If that were true, Kate, I would not have stopped."

She sent a direct look at his distended fly. "Then you're determined to be the king of steel, is that correct?"

Steel would be a more-than-adequate description in terms of his erection, but not when it came to his strength as far as Kate was concerned. "I cannot make love to you Kate. If I do, then I am in danger of hurting you in the process."

"You can't hurt me, Marc. I know what this is all about. Chemistry. Attraction. Not ever-after."

"But you have no idea what my life is about. If anyone even suspects we're involved, you will suffer for it."

"I'm not a wilting flower. And as I told you before, I'm only looking for some adventure." She didn't sound all that convincing. "But I'm not going to force you to do anything you don't want to do."

Right then, he would have gladly taken her down to the floor and finished what they'd started—what he had started. Instead, he turned away and headed for the door.

He needed to remember who he was—a king with a consuming need to be accepted. But his need for Kate was beginning to overshadow everything else.

He could not let that happen. It might destroy everything

he had sought to accomplish in terms of his reputation. But worse, it could destroy her.

Without facing her again, he said, "I will see that Nicholas returns you safely to the hotel."

And then he would retire for the evening, alone, to chastise himself for his complete lack of control.

Even after Marc had been gone for several minutes, Kate could still feel his mouth and hands on her breasts, could still hear him say that he couldn't make love to her, that she was a complication. She refused to be a complication.

Probably just as well he'd stopped, Kate decided as she adjusted her clothing before leaving the office. And she was crazy to think that she didn't want him with every fiber of her being. She did take some comfort in knowing that he wanted her, too. At least from a physical standpoint. Unfortunately, she had tried to fool herself into thinking that she only wanted some adventure with Marc, a few goes at hot and fast lovemaking. In reality, she wanted to be more than his friend, more than his lover. Yet Marc wasn't the kind of man who required more than temporary affairs—without complications.

Kate's feelings for Marc were very complicated and she would have to analyze them later. Right now she needed to put aside her predicament, will away the shakes and see about Cecile. With that thought, she opened the door only to be met head-on by the queen mother.

"Hi, Mary," Kate said in a too-loud voice laden with fake cheerfulness.

"Hello, dear." Mary's gaze roamed over Kate from head to toe. "Have you seen my son?"

Oh, she'd seen him all right, and he had definitely seen her. "He left his office a few minutes ago. How's Cecile?"

"She's an angel and down for her afternoon nap."

Searching for a quick escape, Kate pointed toward the

back staircase leading to the nursery. "I think I'll go check on her now."

"I would prefer you take a walk with me."

Oh, boy. "Any place in particular?"

"The gardens. It's a beautiful day and a good opportunity for us to have a little talk."

Kate assumed her face probably flashed guilt like a billboard, triggering the queen mother's request. Mary most likely suspected something was brewing between Kate and the king. Kate saw no way out aside from running away, but that would further encourage the queen mother's suspicions.

When Kate said, "Lead the way," surprisingly Mary linked her arm with Kate's and guided her down the gilt and marble corridor, then through a pair of double French doors that led to the rear palace grounds.

They remained silent as they strolled along a rock path lined with rose bushes and neatly trimmed hedges. When they reached a stone bench, Mary sat and patted the place next to her. "Join me, Kate."

Kate complied, keeping her gaze trained on a tree where a bluebird flitted along the branches, wishing she could sprout some wings and fly away.

Mary's sigh floated over the gentle breeze. "I suppose you now have the results of Cecile's blood test."

At least she hadn't quizzed her about Marc, Kate thought. But she wasn't sure it was her place to deliver the news that would most likely be a reality jolt. However, she couldn't lie to this woman who had been nothing but kind to her since the beginning. "Yes, I have the results."

"Well?"

Kate shifted until she faced Mary, taking the woman's hand into hers. "Cecile has Philippe's and Marc's blood type."

Mary drew in a long breath and released it on a weary sigh. "Then she is most likely my grandchild."

"Unless there is someone else in the family that could be a possibility."

Mary shook her head. "No. The line ends with Marcel. His father had only one niece, his deceased sister's child, and she is in Canada, happily married with two children. I have no one else in my family."

Kate ached at the loneliness in Mary's voice and grasped for words that might ease her pain. "And now you have Cecile. And Marc."

Mary studied their joined hands. "Marcel has been a stranger to me for the past few years. He's always been searching for something, although heaven only knows what."

"Respect," Kate said with certainty.

"I suppose you're right about that." Mary lifted her gaze to Kate. "Do you believe Cecile is his child?"

"He's adamant that she isn't."

"But do *you* believe him?"

Kate wanted to, honestly she did. "What I think doesn't matter," she said, the same thing she'd told Marc earlier. "Cecile's well-being is important, though. She needs your love."

"She will have it," Mary stated. "I am more concerned with my son. He has much to bear as a king."

"I know, but he has broad shoulders." In both a literal and figurative sense.

"He also needs the love of a good woman."

Kate shrugged. "I'm sure there's a princess somewhere who would be more than willing to give him that."

Mary patted Kate's hand. "My dear, we are running relatively low on monarchs in this day and time. Marcel needs someone who understands him. Someone who can settle him down. A nice, educated woman would fit the bill."

The expectant look on Mary's face took Kate aback. "Again, I'm sure someone will turn his head."

"Someone already has, and that someone is you."

Kate's breath hitched hard in her chest. "Mary, I really don't think—"

"You need not think, Kate. You only need to be there for him. The rest will take care of itself. Unless you do not care for him."

Kate looked away, knowing the guilt had returned. "I'm very fond of Marc. I have been since the day I met him nine years ago."

"But can you love him?"

In many ways, Kate already did. In many ways, she always had. "Right now, Marc needs a friend, and I'm willing to be that to him."

"Friendship is a good place to begin." Mary stared off into space while the afternoon sun washed the gardens in a soft golden glow. "Marcel's father was my friend and my confidant. My lover. The love of my life, even though it was ordained that we marry."

"You mean some sort of arrangement?"

Mary smiled. "I know that must sound archaic to a modern young woman such as yourself. But I tend to believe that fate had a hand in our union. If only fate had not been so cruel as to take him from me much too soon."

The sorrow in Mary's voice, the mist of unshed tears in her eyes, caused a lump to lodge in Kate's throat. After fighting back her own tears, Kate said, "You're still young, Mary. You could find someone else."

"There is no one else for me, my dear. I've loved only one man in my life, a wonderful man, and he has no equal." She drew Kate into an unexpected embrace. "I wish for you that kind of rare and precious love, my dear Kate."

Kate desperately wanted to believe in its existence, but with Marc? Only if he was willing to return that love.

Once they parted, she told Mary, "Thank you. Your story inspires me."

Mary squeezed Kate's hands. "And your presence here is very welcome, which leads me to a request."

"Anything."

"I would like you to move into the palace, or I should say onto the palace grounds." She gestured beyond the path to a break in the hedge. "Over there, you will see a small cottage. Philippe used it as his own private retreat. We've removed his possessions, but it's still nicely furnished. It would afford you some seclusion."

Being so close to Marc both thrilled and concerned Kate. If he decided not pursue a relationship, then she would have to face him on a daily basis, and that could be very detrimental to her heart. "I'll think about it," she promised Mary, and she would think about it, probably most of the night. "In the meantime, I'll be happy to remain here for the next few days to help take care of Cecile."

"That's not necessary, Kate. Beatrice will serve as her nanny. Besides, you will have enough on your plate when you begin your work tomorrow."

"I don't mind missing some sleep where Cecile is involved," Kate insisted. Or where Marc was concerned. "She's such a joy to be around."

Mary stood and stared down at Kate with a knowing look, as if she could read Kate's thoughts. "She is very fond of you, too, Kate. And whether he cares to admit it or not, so is my son."

Six

Marc did not care to admit to himself that what he was feeling for Kate Milner went far beyond simple lust. He admired her conviction, reveled in her strength of will, her insight. Yet he couldn't deny that he longed to make love to her. He also couldn't deny that she was effectively breaking through the armor he had erected to protect his emotions. And he had no idea how he had allowed that to happen.

Yes, he did know. When he was with her, he didn't feel so alone.

But he was alone in his office now, trying to concentrate on work, yet he could only ponder his situation with Kate, memories of their earlier interlude in this very place battering his mind. He could not fall into that trap. Not now. Not with so much riding on his country's expectations of him as a leader. In less than six weeks, he would appear before the governing council to state his case. Doriana needed to move into the twenty-first century, and providing premium health care was of the utmost importance. He had to prove to the ruling body that he had his country's best interests at heart and he needed the funds to see his plans come to fruition.

Now nearing midnight, he tossed aside the proposals he'd been composing for some time and opted to retire to bed. On his way to his suite, he stopped at the nursery to look in on Cecile, hoping to find Kate so he could issue another apology since he had not joined her for dinner. But he only found Cecile, sleeping soundly in the dimly lit, deserted room.

Quietly he approached the crib and stared down at the infant lying on her belly, her knees tucked beneath her and her face turned toward him in profile. Marc watched her for several moments, trying to find something in her features that reminded him of Philippe. She could belong to either one of them based on looks alone. But Marc was very certain she was not his child, even though in many ways he felt responsible for her. After all, Philippe was gone, and she was all that remained of him—if, in fact, Cecile was his child. Deep down, Marc believed that to be the truth. If only he could prove it.

When Cecile released a soft whimper, Marc feared he had inadvertently roused her by his presence alone. He laid his palm on her tiny back and patted her a few moments, praying she would settle back into slumber before she roused Beatrice. Instead, she let go a cry, prompting Marc to pick her up. He walked her around the nursery, soothing her with soft whispers in order not to wake the household.

"You and I will be in a great deal of trouble if you make too much of a fuss," he told her as he retrieved the pacifier from the crib then placed it in her mouth. "Now be a good girl and go back to sleep."

She rubbed her eyes, reared her head back, poked her finger in his mouth then grinned as if to say, "Silly king, I have no intention of sleeping."

How could he resist such a captivating child? He couldn't,

and she knew it. This particular female was determined to wrap his heart around her finger and she was succeeding. So was Kate.

He brushed a kiss across her warm, downy-soft cheek. "Your mother must have held you often, if only we knew who she was."

Cecile yawned, then palmed his jaw as if fascinated by the feel of his whiskers. Without warning, she settled her head on his shoulder.

Marc experienced an unexpected swell of emotion and a fierce protectiveness as he relished her warmth against his heart. She was an innocent, and she deserved the best in life. Even if they never confirmed her parentage, Marc vowed to make certain she was safe, secure and well loved by the family. She would never know the misery of not being accepted.

When he felt she had sufficiently calmed, Marc laid her back in the crib and held his breath. Her eyes opened briefly and she raised her head and leveled her unfocused gaze on him. Then she turned her face away, laid her head back down and her respiration once more became steady and deep.

Marc was greatly satisfied that he had been able to calm her with little effort. If only something so simple could ease him into sleep. If only he had someone to comfort him, to reassure him at times that he wasn't totally floundering as a leader. If only he had Kate to talk to.

But Kate obviously had returned to the hotel, and he would have to face the night alone.

After retiring to his suite, Marc took a quick shower then slipped beneath the cool sheets without bothering to dress. He punched the pillows several times, but couldn't seem to settle down despite his exhaustion.

Turning onto his back, he stared at the ceiling and considered going for a drive. But even that held no real appeal. What he wanted most—what he needed most—was Kate. Odd that he'd spent years without needing anything or anyone, and now in two days' time, he missed her more than he'd missed any human being aside from his father and brother.

Yet he couldn't have a casual affair with Kate; it would have to be all or nothing. And he couldn't consider a serious relationship because, in all honesty, he'd never really had one before. Solid relationships took time to evolve, and at present he did not have an abundance of spare hours. Even though he was expected to marry one day—as Philippe had been expected to—Marc wasn't certain when he'd be ready for that day.

He recalled the wager he had made all those years ago and the reunion with Dharr and Mitch that would take place next spring. The bet had once been a reason to avoid marriage, but now he viewed it as ridiculous ramblings of youth. His reasons to avoid marriage now were much more compelling and complex. And he couldn't let his attraction to Kate sway him, for both her sake and his.

But he did have a yearning for the beautiful doctor that knew no true logic. The remembrance of her kiss, the flush of her breasts, the taste of her against his tongue stirred his body back to life. He rubbed a hand down his bare abdomen, imagining her hand there and much lower. He grew hard as a brick when he fantasized about having her in his bed, sliding into her body, holding her close in his arms. But as much as he desired her physically, he longed more for her trust and respect.

And that could prove to be the greatest challenge of all.

Kate entered the clinic the next morning prepared for her first official day at work. Or as prepared as she could be, considering she'd had relatively little sleep over the past three days. Last night was no exception, thanks to Cecile—and to Marc. But she couldn't be angry with either one of them, especially not after she'd observed Marc's late-night interaction with Cecile. She'd remained hidden in the doorway of the room adjacent to the nursery when she'd heard him come in and watched in fascination as he walked Cecile around the room, comforting her until the baby had finally gone back to sleep. And Marc had left the room not knowing Kate had been there witnessing his care and concern.

To Kate, Marc had seemed like a natural father comforting his daughter. Even if it turned out that he wasn't the father, at least Kate was assured that Marc would step into the role with little effort if necessary.

But right now she had to get her mind on to the business of healing.

After checking in with the clinic's receptionist, Kate was directed to follow Isabella, the nurse who had eyed Marc as if he were chateaubriand during their first meeting. After they entered a small lounge, she told Kate, "You may place your things in the locker," then immediately left, as if she couldn't quite take being in the same room with the new doctor. Maybe she viewed Kate as competition, a ridiculous assumption, Kate decided. She'd never been anyone's competition. And she also needed to remember that the woman's name was not Nurse Lustful so that she wouldn't accidentally slip up.

Kate settled into the routine without much trouble, considering she had acclimated herself to the surroundings the day before. The schedule again was hectic as Kate moved through the exams with Caroline, fueled solely by adrenaline, since she hadn't had the opportunity to have lunch. By the time the afternoon ended, she'd seen almost twenty patients but fortunately she hadn't seen Renault—until she kicked off her shoes and collapsed into the office chair with a cup of weak coffee and a headache that throbbed with each beat of her pulse.

Renault eyed her stocking-covered legs exposed by the skirt she wore, and her bare feet propped on the desk. His perusal made Kate feel as if she'd taken off all her clothes. "Is there something you need, Doctor?" She regretted the words the minute they left her mouth when he sent her a sleazy grin.

"You seem as if you have had a rough day. Perhaps I should ask if there's anything you need from me?"

Your absence. "I'm fine." Kate lowered her feet to the floor and slipped her shoes back on, but she still felt grossly naked due to his continued assessment. "I was just leaving for home."

"Where is home, Dr. Milner?"

How should she answer? She didn't like the thought of mentioning a hotel in the presence of a man who fancied himself a Don Juan. She wasn't too fond of mentioning the palace either, but at least he would realize she had guards at her disposal. Of course, she could say it was none of his business. She opted to affect courtesy and give him a partial truth. "I'm staying at the palace for the time being, until I can find a place of my own."

He took the chair across from her. "I believe there is a cottage available next door to my apartment. It is not far from the hospital."

Living on the other side of the continent from him would be too close for Kate. "Thanks for the suggestion."

"I also have a spare bedroom, if you are interested."

Not on your life. "I don't think that's a good idea."

He nailed her with his demonic eyes. "I believe it would be a very good idea. We could get to know each other better."

"I prefer to keep our relationship on a professional level."

"That is not as enjoyable, *ma chèrie*. But I assure you that my intentions are very honorable."

The scoundrel didn't know the first thing about honor. "Again, I appreciate the offer but I need extra room for myself and my daughter."

Kate picked up her bag and moved from behind the desk, ready for a quick exit until Renault came to his feet and asked, "How is your daughter? Did her laboratory tests turn out well?"

"She's fine. Very healthy. I'll see you tomorrow."

"I find it somewhat coincidental that she looks very much like the DeLoria family. Is there any relation?"

"Of course not," Kate snapped, probably to her own detriment. "Why would you think that?"

"I suppose you could say that I've noticed how the king looks at you. Are you lovers?"

Are you a jackass? "No, we're not lovers. We attended the same university in America. We're friends."

"Only friends?"

"Yes. I need to go."

He moved in closer like a snake in the grass. "First, I would like to say I am pleased you are working with me. Running this clinic can present quite a challenge. At times I wish that I had pursued my goal to become a surgeon."

No one wished that as much as Kate at the moment. "You would've made a good surgeon, I imagine."

"I am flattered, but why would you believe this about me since you have not seen me in action?"

Kate was going to enjoy the heck out of this. "Your hands are made for surgery. Small. Easy to fit into tight spots. And you know what they say about small hands and feet. Guess that's why you tend to overcompensate in other areas."

She headed out the door, smiling all the way down the hall as she reflected on the shock and chagrin on Renault's face.

Little man, big ego, bigger mouth.

After exiting through the service entrance, Kate was surprised to find Mr. Nicholas hadn't arrived to take her back to the palace. When she'd called a few minutes before, he'd said he was on his way. She decided to check the main entrance in case she'd misunderstood his instructions.

She crossed the hospital's vestibule and pushed through the double doors leading outside. Suddenly, hordes of reporters surrounded her, led by one balding, rotund gentleman holding a tape recorder. "Miss Milner, I have a few questions." His English was impeccable but his clothing was not. He looked as though he'd slept in his suit, but then Kate probably didn't look much better.

"*Doctor* Milner," she corrected, craning her neck in hopes of finding the Rolls waiting at the curb to rescue her, but it wasn't to be.

Cameras flashed and videotape rolled when the man said, "Could you please state your relationship with King DeLoria?"

Not again. Why couldn't everyone mind their own business? She had no idea how to handle this situation, but decided honesty would be her best course. After all, she had nothing to hide—except her feelings for the king. She hoped her face wouldn't give her away. "We're former university colleagues."

"Are you lovers?" another man asked.

First Renault, and now this. Where was Marc when she needed him? "We're friends and nothing more."

"Then you deny the rumor that your child was fathered by the king?" one woman shouted from the center of crowd.

Where had that come from? She suspected she already knew the answer. Dear Dr. Renault. "Yes, I deny that," she snapped, then added more sedately, "Before three days ago, when I arrived in Doriana to accept the hospital position, I had not seen King DeLoria in almost a decade."

The bald guy shoved the recorder close to her mouth. "But are you not staying at the palace with him?"

"I'm staying at the inn." Kate breathed a huge sigh of relief when she saw the Rolls pull up. "I have to go now."

She tried to shove her way through the crowd, which was larger now, since several villagers and tourists had stopped to check out the commotion. The crush of people seemed to close in on her with every step, threatening to steal her oxygen as she struggled to reach the bottom of the stairs. Then a hand grabbed her wrist and pulled her forward, while a contingent of bodyguards moved in and attempted to push the onlookers and press corps away.

Marc.

She'd never been so grateful to see anyone in her life. But she didn't reach the safety of the car before one man swung around to capture the king on film and, in doing so, whipped his video camera into Kate's forehead. Her head snapped to one side. Pain shot from the place of impact, bringing tears to her eyes and clouding her vision. Yet she could see well enough to witness Marc drawing back his fist and then landing a punch in the cameraman's nose, sending the man backward into the arms of two guards.

Marc wrapped his arm around Kate's shoulder and herded her through the stunned crowd toward the car where Nicholas stood by, holding open the door and sporting a satisfied smile. "Good show, Your Manliness."

A regular sideshow, Kate thought as Marc ushered her into the car. Only three days spent in this quaint country and she'd already started a riot. Well, she'd wanted some adventure and it looked like she'd gotten it.

Once they were settled into the seat side by side and the door had been closed, Marc leaned forward and told Nicholas, "Take the back route to the palace." Then he hit a button on the console that raised the smoky tinted glass, concealing the rear seat from the driver's view.

Marc turned to Kate, a mixture of anger and concern flaring in his cobalt blue eyes. "How badly are you hurt?"

Kate touched her fingertips to her forehead, right above her left eye. The spot was only slightly tender. "I'm okay. I'll probably just have a bruise for the next few days."

"I'll have Louis come to the palace to examine you."

"I'm a doctor, Marc. Nothing's cracked. No indentation. Just a bump. I have a very hard head."

"Obviously. I will have Dr. Martine examine you regardless," he repeated.

Kate was simply too tired and too rattled to argue. "Suit yourself."

He shifted in his seat and leveled a serious stare on her. "Why were you not waiting at the service entrance?"

Kate bristled at his severe tone. "I went there first. When I didn't find Mr. Nicholas, I decided to check the front in case I was wrong about the location. I had no idea I'd be bombarded with questions."

Marc sighed. "This is my life, Kate. Your connection with me opens you up to scrutiny. What did they ask?"

Kate didn't want to anger him more, but he deserved to know the truth, at least about the impromptu press conference. She would tell him about Renault's speculation later. Much later. "They asked about our relationship. Then they insinuated Cecile is our child, yours and mine, if you can believe that."

Marc reached into the briefcase resting at his side and withdrew a newspaper, then handed it to Kate. "This is where they came up with that theory."

Kate couldn't read a word of the print, but the somewhat blurry photograph of the king carrying a baby into the hospital, a woman by his side—in this case Kate—needed no interpretation.

She tossed the paper aside. "This doesn't prove anything."

Marc turned away and stared out the window. "It's enough to raise suspicions. And damn the vulture who took it."

Kate noticed Marc's hand resting between them, the bruised and puffy knuckles. She caught his wrist and worked his fingers back and forth, all the while watching Marc's face for any signs of pain. He just sat there staring straight ahead, his jaw clenched tight.

"You're going to have some swelling," she said. "But I don't think you've done too much damage. I'm not sure I can

say the same about the camera guy's nose, or your reputation."
She sent him a shaky smile. "I can see the headlines now—
King Saves Damsel in Distress."

"And hopefully will not be charged with assault."

"Can they do that?"

"I'll have my staff deal with it."

Kate allowed a few moments of silence before she said,
"I'm sorry, Marc. I should have been more careful."

He pulled his hand from hers as if he couldn't stand to
touch her. "This isn't your fault. It's mine. I should have prepared you for this."

"How would you do that? Teach me Camera Dodging, 101?"

For a moment she thought he might smile. Instead, he
streaked both hands down his face then his gaze came to rest
on her forehead. "Are you certain you're all right?"

"I'm positive. Promise."

Surprisingly, Marc moved closer and settled one arm along
the back of the seat. "I would not have forgiven myself, Kate,
if something more serious had happened to you. And what did
happen was bad enough."

"It was stupid for me to think that if someone suspected
we were more than friends, it wouldn't really matter."

He took her hand and twined their fingers together. "It
does matter, and I'm the foolish one, Kate."

"Why is that?"

"Because I have inadvertently involved you in this scandal." His intense eyes sent Kate's heart on a marathon. "Because I know I shouldn't do this, but I'll be damned if I can
help myself."

Inclining his head, Marc captured her bottom lip between
his lips before kissing her deeply, tenderly. His mouth melted
into hers like cinnamon candy, a taste she detected on his
tongue that played against hers so sweetly, softly.

For a fleeting moment, Kate rationalized that his kiss was

a result of his frustration and anger, the means to let off steam and the reason why it continued and grew more passionate with every ticking second. But when he slid his palm down her rib cage, to her hip and then back up again, she couldn't lay claim to any rationality for either of them. All she recognized at that moment was a heady warmth oozing from every pore and a desire for Marc DeLoria's full attention that knew no limits.

What else would explain her lack of resistance when he cupped her knee, which was exposed by her skirt that had ridden up to her thighs? What else except a total absence of common sense drove her legs to part in invitation while they were driving in a car? What else could have incited the low moan climbing her throat when he slid his palm beneath the hem of her skirt?

She was very aware of what Marc intended when he kept going until his fingertips hovered at the junction of her thighs. And when he fondled her through the nylon, all thoughts slipped away.

She was growing hotter by the minute, closer and closer to losing it as Marc increased the pressure, both with his mouth firmly joined with hers and his hand working wonders between her thighs. Feeling brazen and bold, she slid her palm up his thigh and to his groin where her fingers contacted the ridge beneath his slacks. She touched him the same way he now touched her, through fabric that created a frustrating obstacle but not enough to stop either one of them from the erotic, forbidden exploration. She didn't think anything could stop them.

"We're here, Your Highness."

The grating sound of Nicholas's voice filtering in from the overhead intercom broke the spell and the kiss. Marc pulled his hand away, slid to the other side of the car and leaned his head back against the seat, his chest rising and falling with his ragged respiration. Kate had trouble catching her breath as well. She already missed his touch, his heat, his mouth that had shown no mercy on her senses.

As they rode through the gates, Marc's rough sigh broke the silence. "My mother told me she offered you the guesthouse. I'll see that your things are brought here."

At least this time he hadn't apologized for losing control since Kate wasn't the least bit sorry. "But won't that be worse, me staying on the grounds?"

"The press probably knows you're at the inn. You'll be afforded more protection here."

The media knew where she was staying because she'd told them, another huge mistake. "If you think that's best for the time being, then I don't have a problem with it."

Marc turned his head toward her. "But we still have one other problem."

"What's that?"

"I'm not strong enough to resist you."

That brought on Kate's smile. "I'll try to behave myself."

"I'm not concerned about your behavior. I am concerned about mine."

Kate was concerned most about her growing feelings for him. "Look, you just punched out a reporter. You can deal with me."

Marc returned her smile with one of his own—a smile that could move the mountains surrounding them. "That is the problem, Kate. I want to deal with you in a very intimate way, and that should be more than obvious to you now. If we had not arrived here when we did, I can promise you I would have done much more, regardless of the fact we were in a moving vehicle with only a glass separating us from prying eyes."

And Kate would have let him.

He leaned over and kissed her cheek immediately before

Nicholas opened the car door. "I'm not certain I will be able to overcome that problem."

Kate sincerely hoped he didn't.

In the middle of the night, after Cecile was tucked safely in bed, Marc escorted Kate to the inn to retrieve her belongings with a bevy of armed guards as their chaperones. Regardless, he'd done well to keep his hands off of her in the privacy of the car, but once they returned to the deserted guest cottage, he questioned how long he could maintain his resolve.

Marc considered leaving her alone, but he truly didn't want to leave, especially after Martine had told him that although Kate's wound didn't appear that serious, someone should watch her in case she showed signs of a concussion.

Presently, she showed Marc a pair of shapely legs encased in nylons as she strolled around the small living room to examine the odds and ends on the bookshelves in the corner. Those damn panty hose had saved him from doing something totally inadvisable earlier that day, before Nicholas had delivered his untimely interruption.

"Another great collection of books," she said, keeping her back to him. "Just wish I could read more French. But I am doing some studying."

Marc was doing some studying of his own—namely the curve of her buttocks and the dip of her waist—as she replaced one volume above her head.

"I could teach you a few words." The words running through his mind now would not be deemed appropriate for common usage. But in bed….

She smiled at him over one shoulder. "I'm doing better at the clinic, picking up a few phrases. I'm sure the more I'm exposed to the various languages, the more I'll learn."

Marc wanted to expose her to more than words. He wanted to expose her to his hands, to his mouth, to his body.

He tried to relax on the floral sofa that now felt as hard and uncompromising as his escalating erection. With every move Kate made, his muscles clenched with the effort to maintain control. But when she turned to him and began pulling the tails of her blouse from the skirt's waistband, he was as hard as he'd ever been in recent memory.

"I think I'll take a shower now," she said.

Marc thought he should show himself to the door before he showed her how much she was affecting him. "Are you feeling well enough to do that?"

"I feel fine."

How well he knew that. "Perhaps I should stand outside the bathroom door in case you should become dizzy."

She strolled to the sofa and stood above him. "Perhaps you should join me in the shower."

He groaned. "I thought you were going to behave."

"I thought you were going back to the palace."

"I am."

"What are you waiting for?"

He waited for his mind to commandeer his libido. Waited for her to toss him out. Waited for logic to come forth and issue a protest strong enough to stop the overpowering need to touch her.

When none of those things happened, Marc caught her wrist and pulled her forward between his parted legs. He slid his hands up her sides, relishing the feel of her curves against his palm, needing to feel more of her, and soon, duty be damned. His reputation be damned. They were alone, and no one would have to know. If he couldn't have all of her, he could at least give her what she needed. He could gain some satisfaction from satisfying her—if that was what she wanted—and he assumed it was, considering her eyes held the cast of desire.

He ran his palms up her thighs, this time beneath the skirt. "I believe I have some unfinished business."

She brushed his hair away from his forehead. "What unfinished business would that be?"

"What I started in the car."

She smiled. "Really? I thought you said—"

"I know what I said. I'm tired of fighting this."

"Then don't fight it."

Marc pulled her down on the sofa into his lap, effectively cutting off all conversation with a kiss that was as intense as the one they'd shared in the car. Kate released an unmistakably sexual sound against his mouth that encouraged him to keep going. She tightened her hold around his neck as he nudged her legs apart and slid one hand along the inside of her thighs, contacting the frustrating barrier bent on keeping him from his goal. Whoever invented panty hose should be bound and gagged with nylon for at least a week.

But that did not deter him. Barriers were made to be broken, and he sufficiently broke through this one with a tug and tear at the seam, revealing she wore nothing beneath them. Kate's gasp didn't stop him either; the press of her hips toward his hand indicated she wanted this as badly as he wanted to give it to her.

Her legs opened more, leaving her completely open to him. Yet as he broke the kiss to watch her face, he considered stopping. He had her at an unfair advantage, and she had him at a crossroad where he greatly questioned his determination not to take her completely, right there, on a sofa. But to stop now would be unimaginable. Not until he gave her the release she deserved, even if he could not have his own.

He found the small bud that blossomed beneath his touch as he caressed her. "Does this feel good?"

Her eyes drifted closed. "It feels…great."

"I cannot argue that," he told her, even as a myriad of arguments against this very thing warred within his conscience. He chose to ignore his concerns and focus only on Kate and her pleasure.

Marc claimed her mouth again as he slid one finger inside her and stroked her, inside and out. He burned to know how it would feel to have her surrounding him when the orgasm claimed her. He settled for only imagining when she climaxed in strong, steady spasms much sooner than he'd expected. But why should that surprise him? They had engaged in enough foreplay to keep them both balanced on the brink of spontaneous combustion.

Had Marc not been resigned to giving Kate only this much, the feel of her might have been his undoing, literally, because in a matter of moments, he could have his slacks undone and his body seated deeply within her heat. His mind insisted he stop now, stop with just this prelude. Instead, he kept touching her, wringing out every last pulse of her climax as he considered giving her another, this time with his mouth…until she said, "I want you, Marc. All of you. Now."

His strength fractured in that moment, even as his mind warned him not to give in. His resistance evaporated completely when Kate moved to his side, released his belt, lowered his zipper, then pulled his slacks and briefs down his hips. She kissed him as she explored him, drove him to the edge with hands as fine as velvet. Marc needed to stop her, that much he knew. He needed to put an end to this madness before it was too late. Before they couldn't stop.

But it was already too late, so at the very least, he needed to make certain he protected Kate against pregnancy.

He caught her wrist and brought her hand up, temporarily ending the torture.

Her eyes narrowed with frustration. "I want this, Marc. So do you."

"We should go to the bedroom, Kate."

"I don't want to wait."

She wrested from his grasp and fumbled with the buttons on her blouse, then slipped it away along with her bra. Marc wasn't sure he would make it to the bedroom when Kate stripped out of her skirt and ruined panty hose, then tossed them away. Now she was beautifully naked, and completely his. After tearing off his own shirt and kicking off his slacks, he bent, reached into his pants' pocket and withdrew the condom he'd brought with him, knowing all along this would probably happen. Hoping all along that it would.

After he had the condom in place, Kate stretched out on the sofa and held out her arms to him. He gladly eased into her embrace, eased into her body and experienced a freedom he hadn't known in years. It had nothing to do with the length of time since he'd been in a woman's arms. It had everything to do with Kate Milner and the hold she had on him. For a moment, the guilt tried to come forth, but he pushed it aside as he put himself at the mercy of nature and his need for Kate.

Marc moved in a slow cadence at first until the chemistry that had been flowing between them exploded in a wild, reckless rhythm. He slid his hands over Kate's body as if he could not get enough of the feel of her. She raked her hands down his back and molded them to his buttocks as he drove harder, faster, losing all sense of time and place in pursuit of pleasure. When he felt the first ripples of Kate's climax, Marc drew one crested nipple into his mouth, sending her over the edge and drawing him farther into her body. Not long after, he joined her with a jolt and a shudder that he couldn't control any more than he could temper his pounding heart. He regretted it had happened too quickly, had been over too soon. Right now he felt too damn good to ruin the moment with any other regrets.

They remained twined together in a tangle of limbs, their bare flesh slick with their efforts and their breathing broken and heavy. Marc buried his face in Kate's hair and savored the feel of her hands stroking his back, their bodies still closely joined. He could stay this way forever and say to hell with the world, to his responsibilities and the problems facing him.

The shrill of the phone splintered the silence and sent Marc up and away from Kate as if he'd been caught red-handed by the royal court.

Kate leaned over him to grab the phone from the end table, rubbing her breasts across his chest, eliciting his groan.

She fumbled for the phone and answered with a breathless, "Hello," then sent Marc a forlorn look. "Hi, Mary. No, you didn't interrupt anything. I was just about to take a shower."

Marc mouthed, "Do not tell her I'm here," but realized it was too late when Kate said, "He's here. We've just returned from the inn with my things. He's about to leave."

Marc rose from the sofa, snatched his clothing from the floor and headed to bathroom while Kate told his mother, "If it's okay, I'm going to get dressed first and take a quick bath. I mean, undressed and take a bath, then I'll be up to see if I can get her to sleep."

Marc was quite up again and doubted he would be sleeping at all.

After dressing, he returned to Kate and found her wearing only her blouse that came to the tops of her thighs. "Nothing like a fussy baby to interrupt," she said, looking self-conscious.

Marc streaked a hand over his nape. "It was a timely interruption, otherwise we might have gone to your bed, and that would have been unwise, considering I only have one condom."

She walked to him and circled her arms around his waist. "It would have been wonderful, and the night isn't over yet, unless you don't have any more condoms in your room."

Held captive by her body molded to his, he slid his hands down her back and palmed her bare bottom. They came together in another earthshattering kiss until reality and regret tunneled their way into Marc's brain.

He pulled her arms away and stepped back. "I can't offer you anything beyond lovemaking, Kate. Not at this point in my life."

She lifted her chin a notch. "If you tell me that one more

time, I'm going to scream. I don't expect anything from you, Marc. And I don't believe you didn't want this to happen."

He'd definitely wanted it, more than he should. "I certainly didn't want to be king, but that decision has been forced upon me."

She looked despondent and Marc wished he could take back his thoughtless words. "Are you saying I forced you to do this?"

"Of course not, and you should realize that. My only regret involves the chaos my life has become. You do not deserve that."

Kate frowned. "Why don't you let me decide what I do and don't deserve. And as far as you being king, why don't you try and concentrate on the good you're doing?"

"Sometimes I wonder if I am doing anything right."

"You are." She touched his face with reverence, as if she believed in him. "I know firsthand what it's like to have people depending on you. My parents are very needy and I couldn't take it anymore. That's why I came here, to get away and make my own life."

He took her hand and kissed her palm before releasing it. "But I cannot walk away." At times, he wished he could.

"No, you can't, but you can focus on the positive aspects of your power and skills." She winked and grinned. "I've certainly experienced a few."

His body lurched back to life. "Kate, you have no idea what you do to me when you make those statements."

She ran a slow fingertip down the ridge beneath his fly. "Yes, I do." She returned to the couch, retrieved the panty hose, balled them up and then tossed them at Marc. "Here's a little souvenir of our night together, so you don't forget."

As if Marc could really forget something that had been so incredible.

With a wicked smile, Kate turned and walked down the

corridor leading to the bath, leaving Marc holding her ruined panty hose while he clung to his last vestiges of sanity. He recognized it was only a matter of time before they made love again, unless he developed a steel will. He did not foresee that happening, considering he now knew how good it had felt to be inside of her, to be totally lost in her.

Yet it was Kate's understanding of the man beneath the king that had begun to appeal to him on a deeper, distinct level beyond carnality. As a king, he feared disappointing his people—and as a man, he feared disappointing Kate. Not when it came to lovemaking; he had always been confident in that regard. They were good together. Damn good. But could he be the man that she needed, the one she would want for all time? And could he give all of himself to her, even the part he had kept hidden from the world? Kept hidden from himself?

If he made a commitment to explore more than their mutual desire, he would have to follow through, since Kate merited a man who would give her all his attention and consideration. While before he would have rejected that prospect, he was actually beginning to consider all the possibilities—and advantages—of having Kate Milner in his life.

Seven

Kate Milner had done the unthinkable. She'd fallen in love with Marc DeLoria all over again.

Oh, she'd tried to convince herself that all she'd wanted was a little adventure with Marc. For that reason, she'd been playing the primo seductress when, in fact, she wanted his heart as much as she wanted his body. And three nights ago, he'd proven to her that he was the consummate lover—and a man who had no designs on being tied to a serious relationship.

How many women had fallen hopelessly in love with him, only to be left behind? She couldn't begin to imagine, but she also wasn't ready to give up. Some day, someone was going to lay claim to his heart. Why not her?

Because the only commitment that interested Marc was his commitment to his kingdom. Kate was a diversion, someone to keep his mind off his troubles during a few stolen moments. Yes, he'd said he respected her, thought she was special, even beautiful, but he hadn't mentioned anything about his feelings for her beyond that. It was crazy for her to expect anything else, especially since she hadn't seen much of him at all for the past few days. Once more, he'd become the elusive king, choosing to keep himself secluded doing heaven only knew what. She only knew that it hadn't involved her.

She had to accept the realization that their one night together might be all that they would ever share. Had to accept she would probably be one of many women who had tried to win him over, without success.

At least her day at the clinic had been relatively successful, and somewhat quieter than the past few days. But unfortunately, that had allowed her time to think about Marc and worry about how long she would continue to hope that her relationship with him might evolve into more. That wouldn't happen if he continued to avoid her. At least his mother and Cecile had been great company. Although she'd enjoyed being with them, it wasn't the same thing as having time alone with Marc.

She was simply too tired to think about it at the moment. Now nearing 6:00 p.m., she'd seen her last patient an hour ago and had remained to catch up on some paperwork before she called Mr. Nicholas for her ride back to the guesthouse. One thing she did know—she would never, ever go near the front entrance again, even though Marc had ordered guards posted at every access. And she felt somewhat guilty that that had been necessary.

Kate charted the last of her notes at the desk in the small office Dr. Martine had arranged for her this morning. At least she was out of Renault's line of fire now, with the exception of passing him in the hall. And at least he hadn't tried to make a pass. Otherwise, she might have introduced her knee to his family jewels.

The sound of voices startled Kate, since she assumed she was alone in the clinic. A woman's voice and a man's voice—namely, the queen mother's and the king's.

Kate pushed back from the desk and opened the door to

find them standing outside the office, both looking extremely distressed.

Panic settled on Kate's chest. "Is something wrong with Cecile?"

Mary attempted a smile. "Oh, no, dear. Cecile is fine. She's with Beatrice."

"Then why are you here?"

"Because of this." Marc held up another newspaper. "Aside from my show of temper with the cameraman, it covers the 'palace baby' and cites an anonymous source who claims he or she has proof that the child is yours and mine."

Kate closed her eyes and pinched the bridge of her nose between her thumb and pointer finger. "I was afraid this might happen."

"This is not your fault, Kate," Mary said. "The media know no restraint where our family is concerned. Some people delight in creating false rumors to discredit us."

Kate looked up to see indisputable anger in Marc's expression and regretted not telling him about Jonathan's comments. "The source is probably Renault. He made the first insinuations three days ago."

Marc's eyes narrowed. "Why did you not tell me after this happened?"

"Because I didn't want to upset you further."

"You can bloody well believe I am upset."

"Settle down, Marcel," Mary scolded. "Kate does not deserve your anger. She was only doing what she thought was best for you."

Kate turned her attention to Mary because it was too painful to look at Marc. "Is there anything I can do? Maybe an interview?"

Mary gave her a sympathetic look. "No, my dear. We will have to allow this gossip to run its course until we can come up with our own retraction."

"Or the proof that Cecile is Philippe's child," Marc added.

"And what purpose would that serve?" Mary asked.

"To clear Kate's name. And mine."

Kate felt as if she were being pulled into a human tug-of-war. "Don't worry about me, Marc. I can cope with this."

He sent her a hard look. "Can you?"

Mary wrapped her arm around Kate's shoulder and gave her a squeeze. "She most certainly can, Marcel. Kate is a mature, strong woman. I have no doubt she will deal with the situation with grace."

Kate wished she had Mary's confidence. "I'll do whatever you instruct me to do. I promise I won't speak to anyone without consulting you first."

"Of course, dear. We trust you. We simply wanted to forewarn you and have Marcel escort you back to the palace." Mary dropped her arm from Kate's shoulder and stared at Marc. "And you will be courteous to the doctor. In the meantime, I will return home to check on our charge. I'm certain Beatrice would appreciate someone to relieve her."

Kate saw her chance to escape. She didn't want to talk to Marc until he'd had time to calm down. "Give me a minute and I'll be ready to go. I can help."

"I need to see you first. Alone."

Marc's command caused Kate to stiffen from the fury she sensed building just below the surface of his composed demeanor. She wasn't afraid of Marc; she was afraid she couldn't find the words to reason with him. But she had to try.

"Okay. I can do that," she said.

"Take your time," Mary said as she headed away. "I will tell the guards to remain posted outside and have Nicholas return for you after he has delivered me to the palace."

Once Mary was out of sight, Kate gestured toward the office. "Let's go in here so we can have some privacy."

Marc stepped inside the room and reclined against the

desk, arms folded across his chest. Kate closed the door and leaned back against it for support.

"You should have told me about Renault. We might have prevented the rumors from escalating, or at least been better prepared."

"The damage was already done by the time the press got to me," Kate said. "And again, I didn't say anything about Renault because I knew you had already reached the boiling point."

"It's been three days, Kate. You could have told me in that length of time."

Her own anger rose to the surface. "How was I supposed to do that? You haven't been around. It's hard to tell someone something when that someone refuses to talk."

"I've had a lot on my mind."

"So have I, Marc."

"I know. And that, too, is my fault." His anger melted into resignation. "I should probably claim Cecile is my child and allow the council to do as they see fit with me."

Kate was only now beginning to recognize that a scandal of this proportion—real or fabricated—could do irrevocable injury to Marc's standing as a leader. She should have realized that he was no different from any man in power, even if he had been born into the responsibility. "They can't oust you, can they?"

"No, but they can make it difficult for me to accomplish anything from this point forward. I rely on their complete support. Without it, I am only a figurehead."

"Then fight them."

"What would be the point?"

Kate sent him an incredulous look. "What would be the point? Because you're good at what you do. Because you want to make your country a better place. You care about your people. Everyone knows that."

"You're making a huge assumption."

Stubborn man. "I'm not illiterate, Marc. I read the papers. I've followed your rise to power. I know how much you've been admired in your diplomatic endeavors, and your recent reputation as a strong leader."

"You've forgotten my reputation of being a womanizer. That seems to have taken precedence in my adulthood."

"Until Philippe died. Since then, you've gained respect from world leaders."

"I've achieved nothing, Kate, at least in the eyes of my people. They will not forgive this."

Kate threw up her hands and released a frustrated sigh. "Okay, Marc. Give up, if that's what you want to do. I'm certainly not going to stop you. Just don't expect me to stand by and watch you self-destruct."

Though it was the hardest thing she'd ever done, Kate turned away from him. She saw no sense in trying to convince him to fight, not when he seemed so against undertaking the battle—one he would have to face alone, by his choice.

Kate only got as far as the door when Marc slammed his palm against the facing, preventing her from opening it. "I need you to understand, Kate."

She turned and saw a pain in his eyes that stole her breath. "I do understand, Marc, more than you give me credit for. I just can't stand the thought of you throwing in the towel. You can't back down now, not when you have so much to lose."

"Right now, I would gladly walk away, but you're right. I owe it to my country to fight. I owe it to Philippe's memory."

"You owe it to yourself, Marc. This is only a temporary situation. We'll get through it together. We're both strong enough, and we're a good team."

He touched her face with tenderness. "I don't know what I have done right in this lifetime to have you on my side, especially after the way I've treated you of late. And I am sorry for that."

"I know. I also know you're a good man with a huge burden to bear. And you'll be a good father to Cecile. She needs you, too, even if she's not your child."

"And I need you. More than you realize."

Kate waited to experience the suffocation, the resentment of someone needing her. It didn't come.

She doubted Marc was inclined to ask for help very often—partly from pride and partly from trying to prove he could go it alone. The admission seemed to be costing him a lot, evident in the uneasiness in his expression. And if she could help him, she would. She loved him that much.

"I'm here for you, Marc." At least for now. "But you have to let down your guard and let me in."

He tipped his forehead against hers. "You're the only sanity in my life, Kate, and I want you so badly at times it hurts. That's why I've avoided you, knowing that every time I look at you…touch you…every time…"

He kissed her then—a passionate kiss that exposed his desperation, his need, causing the carpeted floor to sway beneath Kate's feet. Without breaking the kiss, Marc spun her around and guided her back until she felt the desk nudge her bottom. He pressed against her, letting Kate know exactly how much he needed her, setting her senses on maximum alert and sending her pulse on a sprint. He slid his hands over her body, from shoulders to hips and then back up to fondle her breasts through her beige silk blouse.

He undid her slacks and slipped his hand inside, touching her as if starved for the intimate contact. He made her body weep with every caress of his fingertips, made her give everything over to the sensations he evoked so masterfully. Kate trembled from the onslaught of feelings, from the love she'd kept hidden from him and probably always would.

Before the climax completely took hold, Marc took his hand away yet kept his mouth mated firmly with hers. She didn't have to ask what he was doing when she heard the metallic sound of his belt buckle release and the track of his zipper.

They shouldn't do this, Kate thought. Not here, not now, not without…

Marc pushed her slacks and underwear to her thighs then pushed into her with a hard thrust. Her body responded with an all-consuming climax that nearly brought her to her knees, saved only by Marc's hold on her. Her mind now trapped in a carnal web, Kate could no longer think coherently as Marc set a frantic rhythm, his hands molded to her bottom, pulling her closer, moving in deeper and deeper.

He finally ended the kiss and brought his lip to her ear, whispering something in French…a low, deep declaration that set her imagination on fire.

His respiration increased and his heart pounded against her chest. With one last thrust, his frame went rigid in her arms and he shook with the explosive force of his own climax.

She kissed his face, stroked his hair, held him close as their breathing returned to normal. But the return of awareness of what had happened—and what they hadn't done—hit Kate with the force of an earthquake. She'd wanted to absorb his pain, escape their problems and make more memories—only to disregard the one thing that had been necessary to prevent creating more havoc in both their lives.

She knew the moment reality hit Marc when he muttered a harsh curse in English, one she had no trouble understanding. He braced his hands on the table on either side of her and kept his eyes lowered. "We didn't—"

"I know."

"Can you—"

"Get pregnant?" she finished for him. "Yes."

"Bloody hell."

Kate had mistakenly envisioned Marc's words of love, not words of regret, after the tender moments they'd shared before this uncontrolled act. How ridiculous of her to think such a thing. How stupid of her to be so careless. She was a doctor. She knew the possible consequences, but so did Marc.

His remorse became all too clear when he slipped from her body and turned his back on her. "I do not expect your forgiveness for my total disregard for caution," he said as he redid his slacks.

She couldn't disregard the emotional wall he had erected, his distant tone.

Kate adjusted her clothes with trembling hands, unable to shake the seriousness of the situation. She hoped an attempt at humor might defuse the situation. "Well, we can now add offices to our list of places to avoid, along with sofas and kitchens. Maybe if we just sleep together in a bed, we'll be able to control ourselves."

When he faced her again, Marc's stony expression told Kate her efforts hadn't worked. "It doesn't matter where we are, Kate. The only way we'll avoid losing control is by avoiding each other. I can only assure you that I've never been this irresponsible. Never. It seems all I do is create one problem after another."

Kate should be flattered by the fact that she'd driven him to such abandon, but she wasn't, considering what it might mean in the long term. Considering he saw her—their lovemaking—as a problem, when she considered it a gift. "Look, if I happen to be pregnant, I don't expect anything from you. But you have my guarantee I'll love any child that belongs to me, whether you choose to be involved in its life or not."

Anger turned his eyes as dark as moonless midnight. "Do you believe so little of me that you think I would abandon my own child? If that is so, then it would stand to reason that you don't believe my claims that Cecile is not my child."

Could things get any worse? "I do believe you, Marc. I just don't want you to feel obligated to do anything you don't want to do. And if you think we should avoid each other, then all you have to do is tell me. I won't bother you again."

"Kate, I want…" He hesitated then spun around and headed to the door. "Nicholas is probably waiting. I'll ride back with one of the guards. We can discuss this later."

Kate fought back a sudden rush of tears as she followed him into the hall. "Marc, we need to talk about this now. You can't just walk away."

"Are the king and his lady having a lovers' quarrel?"

Kate and Marc turned simultaneously toward the end of the corridor. Mortification set in when Kate realized the annoying voice belonged to none other than Jonathan Renault.

How could they deny his allegations now?

Marc chose not to fight the sudden fury welling within him. In fact, he welcomed the wrath that he now directed at Renault with an acrid look, his hands fisted at his sides itching to wipe the smug look off the doctor's face. "You are treading on dangerous ground, Renault. You have been since you made your erroneous assumptions known to the press."

Renault looked Kate up and down before centering on her flushed face and kiss-swollen lips. "It seems my assumptions have been correct, although I assure you I've said nothing to the press."

Marc took a menacing step forward. *"Menteur."*

"I am a liar? Forgive me, Your Highness, but are you not guilty of the same? You have lied about your relationship with Dr. Milner. Of course, I do understand your motivation. I cannot imagine the people of Doriana would accept that their king had taken a common *putain* as his lover."

No one called Kate a whore. No one. "You low-life bastard." Rage sent Marc forward but before he could land a fist on Renault's ugly face, Kate grabbed his arm. "No, Marc," she said. "This will only make matters worse."

"Listen to your lover, Your Highness," Renault said, cowering in the corner of the corridor. "I will press charges with the authorities if you lay one hand on me. I do not care if you are the king."

Marc derived some satisfaction in the terror calling out from Renault's eyes. "You're right. I am not above the law. But I am within my rights to dismiss you from your position. I expect you to vacate the premises tonight and not return. And if I see you again, I won't be so benevolent."

"Are you threatening me, King Marcel?"

"I am saying I will no longer tolerate your insolence, Renault."

"And I promise you will regret your decision."

After the doctor scurried away, Marc crouched in the hall and grabbed his nape with both hands. He couldn't remember feeling so drained and useless. He'd always shown great restraint when dealing with the likes of Renault and practicing care when it came to lovemaking. Tonight he had done neither.

He felt a gentle touch on his head. "Let's go home, Marc."

Home.

Marc didn't feel as if he really had a home, a place where he truly belonged, at least not one where he was welcome…except when he'd been in Kate Milner's arms.

Two days had gone by since the clinic fiasco and Kate had barely seen Marc except in passing. Again. She'd occupied her time with work and searching hospital records for any mysterious women who'd given birth six to eight months before, as Marc had requested. Yet she hadn't come across any information that might lead to the identity of Cecile's mother. All the children had been accounted for through pediatric follow-ups except for one, and that had been a boy. Most likely that child's family had moved away, and it began to look as if Cecile had not been born at St. Simone's hospital after all, which greatly complicated the investigation.

Kate decided she would have to start questioning the staff, if she could even begin to concentrate on anything aside from Marc's troublesome, self-imposed withdrawal. Right now, she had to feed a very fussy Cecile.

"I am worried about my son."

Kate looked up and centered her gaze on Mary. Obviously his mother shared her concern. "Marc's worried about everything." She made silly airplane noises while trying to slip the spoon of strained carrots into Cecile's smiling mouth.

Mary reached over and swiped at the baby's face after Cecile blew a raspberry, sending the orange pureed food all over Kate's T-shirt. "He has much to be concerned about, but he will get through this with you by his side."

Kate sensed Marc wanted nothing to do with her now, and that made her hurt in the worst way, right in the area of her heart. "He'll get through it by himself. He's a very strong man."

Mary smiled a mother's smile. "A very strong man who is fighting falling in love every step of the way."

Kate spoke around her shock, with effort. "Mary, I hope you're not misunderstanding mine and Marc's relationship. We're just friends." Her declaration had a false ring to it, and she figured Mary had seen right through the pretense.

"I do not presume to know anything, Kate. However, when he looks at you, his heart shines from his eyes. Have you not noticed this?"

No, she hadn't. She'd only seen regret and anger. The past few days during their limited contact during dinner, she'd seen nothing at all. "He's mad at me. It doesn't have anything to do with love."

"He's angry at the world, Kate. He's in love with you."

Needing an escape, Kate rose from the table, cleaned Cecile's hands and face then slid her from the high chair. "I'm going to put this little one to bed after her bath."

"Beatrice can do that, dear. You look as though you might collapse from exhaustion."

True, every one of Kate's muscles protested the least bit of activity, but that had to do with some very strenuous love-making in some less-than-comfortable positions, even though it had been days since her last interlude with Marc.

Heat traveled up her throat to her face when the images came to mind. "I'll put the baby to bed. It will give Beatrice a break and me a chance to wind down after a long day."

Mary's grin was surprisingly wicked for a sophisticated queen mother. "I can think of other ways to do that."

Kate frowned. "I'm not sure what you mean."

"Yes you do, and so does my son. But if you prefer to play innocent, I'll certainly understand. One does not normally discuss matters of an intimate nature with one's future mother-in-law."

Kate's eyes opened wide and so did her mouth. "You're kidding, right?"

Mary rose with stately grace and patted Kate's cheek, then Cecile's. "I would never make light of something so important. And I have very good instincts about these things. I only hope that you do as well."

Mary sashayed away, her red silk caftan flowing behind her. She smiled at Kate over her shoulder before she disappeared out the door.

Kate took a moment to absorb Mary's outrageous assumptions. Wrong assumptions, at least about a marriage between her and Marc. But she hadn't been wrong about their relationship progressing beyond friendship, at least for Kate. Mary was mistaken to think that her son was at all interested in settling down, not with the weight of the kingdom resting on his shoulders.

"Isn't that a silly idea, Marc wanting to marry little old me?" Kate asked Cecile as she headed to the nursery.

Cecile blew a bubble and belly laughed.

Kate hugged her hard. "My sentiments exactly."

Again Marc found himself locked in his suite, attempting to lock out his problems. For the past few days, he'd met with advisers and his press aide to try to counteract the allegations. But the speculation involving his relationship with Kate and Cecile's parentage had already reached most of Europe. Nothing like a royal scandal to wake the world.

He'd also successfully pushed Kate away, and he regretted that decision even if it was best for them both. He had battled the urge to go to her, make love with her, lose himself in her and in doing so recapture some of his strength. Yet he couldn't keep relying on her to serve as his proverbial port in a storm. He'd never relied on anyone to see him through his problems. Except for Kate, he realized when he reflected on their first encounters, her assistance with his studies all those years ago. But since that time, he'd been on his own. He would continue to make it on his own. Alone.

But he had found some solace during a few late-night meetings with little Cecile. He could basically set his watch to the exact moment when she would wake and require soothing, half-past midnight. Several times he'd almost laughed when he'd heard Beatrice telling his mother that the baby was now sleeping through the night. But his laughter did not come easily these days.

He glanced at the bedside clock and realized the time for Cecile to rouse was upon him now. He might not be able to establish a solid role as a leader to suit everyone concerned, or give Kate all that she needed beyond physical pleasure, but he could at least play the part of white knight to an innocent child. A child who looked to him for nothing more than company, looked at him with admiration, without judgment, when he rescued her pacifier from the floor.

After shrugging on his robe, he walked quietly through the hallway to the nursery and opened the door. Instead of finding the room totally deserted, he discovered Cecile cradled in Kate's arms, both sound asleep in the rocker.

Marc leaned a shoulder against the door and watched them with a warmth that radiated from his soul and settled on his heart. Kate's face looked tranquil and beautiful in sleep. He wanted to put Cecile to bed, then carry Kate to his bedroom. He settled for staring a few more moments, then closed the door behind him.

He leaned back against the wall outside the room and stared at the ceiling. He could not fight his feelings for Kate any longer. He cared deeply for her, more than he had for any woman. And he wanted to be with her, regardless that he shouldn't.

Determination sent him back to his suite to plan. He would somehow make it up to Kate, do something to show her how much he did care.

If, in fact, she still wanted him.

Kate really wanted to holler like a maniac.

If one more person asked if she was the king's girlfriend, then she would let go a yell that would be heard across the ocean. Her mother had been the latest in the long line of inquiring minds during their recent conversation. Kate had told her that she and Marc were just friends, not exactly the truth but not really a lie, at least not now. They hadn't been much of anything for the past five days.

Kate needed a break from it all, from the gossip and innuendo and sideways glances. Today was Saturday, a much-needed day off, and she prepared to spend some of her time talking with the staff about Philippe DeLoria. If she happened to come upon any relevant information, then she would have an excuse to talk to Marc. Otherwise, she refused to invade his privacy since he seemed determined to steer clear of her. Eventually, she did intend to confront him, but not until she knew exactly what she would say.

Following a meager lunch, Kate made her way through the gardens and entered the palace through the kitchen, coming upon Beatrice preparing several of Cecile's bottles. A good place to start with her inquiry, Kate decided. After all, they'd become fast friends, and the nanny did speak decent English.

"Hi, Bea," Kate said, bringing forth the nanny's smile over the pet name Kate had given her.

Beatrice swiped a forearm across her forehead, where wayward tendrils of auburn hair rained down from her neat bun. "Hello, Dr. Kate. If you are looking for the baby, she is sleeping. The queen mother is also taking a nap."

Kate took a stool at the kitchen workstation across from Beatrice and immediately thought about the first time Marc had kissed her by the stove. They'd come a long way in a short time, and they still had far to go—if Kate had any say in the matter.

Pushing those thoughts aside, she said, "Actually, I wanted to talk with you, Bea. Did you know Philippe?"

Beatrice didn't look up from screwing the cap on to one of the bottles. "Yes, ma'am, I did know him."

"Then you worked here before he died?"

"Yes, ma'am."

"How well did you know him?"

Beatrice's gaze snapped up, her hazel eyes wide with horror. "I did not know him in *that* way, mademoiselle."

Her strong reaction made Kate question if the woman was telling the absolute truth, but then Beatrice was a year away from forty and didn't seem like the kind who would take a younger man as a lover. However, nothing would surprise

Kate these days. "I'm not saying you and King Philippe were close in that way. I'm just wondering if maybe he was involved with a woman. Someone the family might not have known about."

Beatrice fumbled with a bottle, barely saving it from a major formula spill. "He was engaged to marry Countess Trudeau."

Kate suspected the woman's nervousness could indicate knowledge of a secret tryst. She bent her elbow and leaned her cheek against her palm. "What was she like, the countess?"

"I have never met her."

"Then she wasn't around all that much."

"No." Beatrice picked up the bottles and put them in the refrigerator before coming back to Kate. "I must go and check on the baby."

Kate rested her hand on Beatrice's arm. "I know you probably don't want to answer my questions, Bea, but this is very important. You can trust that whatever you tell me will be protected."

"I do not understand what you are asking of me."

"I think you know something about Philippe DeLoria's love life. Did he have a secret lover?"

Beatrice twisted the white apron she wore over her plain gray shift. "I could not say... I should not..."

"I have to know, Bea. This could help us find Cecile's mother."

The nanny glanced around the room like a frightened doe, then turned her attention to back to Kate. "If I tell you, will you vow not to tell the queen mother the information came from me? I have been sworn to secrecy when it comes to the royal family's privacy."

Kate raised her hand in oath. "I promise."

After looking around the room once more, Beatrice leaned forward and whispered, "It was rumored he had a lover in one of the mountain villages, a peasant girl. I think I saw her once, in the guesthouse late at night. I was…" Her gaze faltered. "I was going for a walk with a friend in the gardens."

Kate was curious about Beatrice's little late-night rendezvous with the *friend,* but that wasn't the main issue. "Can you describe her to me?"

"I could not see her."

"Do you know her name? Even her first name would help."

"No. I heard him call her *mon amour.* My love. That was all."

And it was more information than they'd had to this point. Kate circled the counter and drew Beatrice into a quick hug. "Thank you, Bea. You're the best."

"And so are you, Dr. Kate. You bring joy to the household."

If only that were true, Kate thought. At least where Marc was concerned. "Have you seen King DeLoria?"

"Bernard…" Beatrice blushed like the devil. "I mean Mr. Nicholas said that the king would be gone most of the day."

Bernard and Beatrice. Maybe that mystery was solved. If only Kate could say the same for the mystery mother, and Marc's activities over the past few days. Maybe he had found a lover in a mountain village. Kate burned over that thought.

"Could you have Mr. Nicholas tell the King I need to see him, Bea? I'll be waiting in the guesthouse."

"As you wish, Doctor."

"Just Kate. I think we should be on a first-name basis now."

Beatrice beamed as if Kate had offered her the queen's palace suite. "I would like that very much, at least when we are in private. Otherwise, it would not be respectful."

Kate shrugged. "That's fine. I'll see you later. And thanks for everything."

With a newfound energy, Kate strode through the gardens, stopping to smell the roses lining the path. She skipped the last few yards like a schoolgirl and burst into the guesthouse, pulling up short when she found Marc sitting on the elegant wingback chair in the corner next to the white brick fireplace, looking dark and imposing against the pristine backdrop, and incredibly sexy in his faded jeans and black knit shirt.

"Where have you been?" His voice was low, demanding.

Kate refused to fall at his feet, although it was tempting. "What does it matter to you? You haven't been all that concerned over my whereabouts for the past week."

"I've been busy."

"So have I." She started to tell him about the conversation with Beatrice but words escaped her when he kept staring as if he really wanted to get her naked. And she really wanted to let him.

But first and foremost, she had to maintain some control in his presence. His recent rejection still stung and she needed to resist him.

"Why are you here?" Her timid voice betrayed her conviction.

"You need to accompany me on a drive," he said.

She snapped her fingers. "Just like that?"

"Yes."

"I'm supposed to drop everything?" Her clothes immediately came to mind.

"It would be in your best interest to accompany me."

Of all the arrogant kings. "And what if I don't?"

At least this time she sounded more confident. But Kate's confidence scattered when Marc came to his feet slowly, his eyes burning holes in her fake bravado. He stalked toward her until he stopped immediately in front of her, so close she could trace the outline of his Adam's apple. "Do you really wish me to show you what I'll do if you do not agree?"

Kate dared him with a look. "If you think you're man enough."

Proving he was very much a man—a Cro-Magnon man—Marc grabbed her and tossed her over his shoulder, then headed out the open door. He took away her breath when he set her in the all-terrain vehicle and slid his tongue across her lower lip. Then he took away her sight when he covered her eyes with a strip of white cloth, brushing one breast with a fingertip after he was done.

As ridiculous as it seemed, Kate didn't care what he did as long as he eventually removed the blindfold—and anything else he cared to remove.

So much for resisting him.

Eight

"**H**ow much farther?"

"It won't be long now."

Marc glanced at Kate, who seemed extremely sedate for someone wearing a blindfold. Although the pastoral terrain offered a panoramic view, the less she knew of their destination, the better. He wanted to save the full effect of the scenery for when she first encountered four thousand square feet of natural wood structure, set among ancient forests and majestic mountains, miles from any significant population, at least during the summer, before the arrival of snow.

He intended to use the remainder of the weekend to treat Kate as she deserved to be treated, to make love to her undisturbed in a real bed in the glow of firelight. To tell her what he was feeling. As far as Marc was concerned, his own private retreat would aid in accomplishing that goal, if Kate chose to cooperate.

After pulling into the narrow drive, Marc shut off the Hummer and opened his door. "We're here."

"Where is here?"

When Kate reached for the knot on the cloth, he told her, "Do not take that off yet."

She wrinkled her upturned nose. "Why not?"

He leaned over and whispered, "Because I want to remove it." He anticipated taking off more than the blindfold before evening's end.

After sliding from the seat, he rounded the vehicle then helped her out. The afternoon sun enhanced the chestnut highlights in her hair and, when he untied the cloth, illuminated her deep green eyes that revealed surprise and something he couldn't quite name, but it almost resembled anger.

Without speaking, she surveyed the pines surrounding the lodge for a few moments then climbed the steps leading to the porch that spanned the length of the building. She faced him again, her hands clasped behind her back as she rocked on her heels. "This must be the infamous cabin."

Infamous? Obviously the staff had been talking, Marc decided.

He passed by her and inserted the key into the lock, disappointed over her lack of enthusiasm. "I see that someone has ruined my surprise. Was it Nicholas?"

"Actually, it was Elsa."

Marc's hand froze on the doorknob. "Elsa?"

"During our phone conversation, she asked me if you'd taken me to the 'little' cabin yet, although I can't say that I agree with her definition of 'little.'"

Damn Elsa and her cavernous mouth. Marc would like to find a phone to give her a piece of his mind. But no phones were available here, a very good thing in his opinion. No phones, no interruptions. Unless Kate now demanded that he take her back to civilization. He planned to prevent that from happening, or at least try.

Marc pushed the door open, stepped to one side and considered Kate's entry into the cabin without coercion a small victory. Very small when he noted the continued absence of eagerness in her expression.

He decided the best course would be honesty when it came to his past. "I brought Elsa here only once. My mother was getting on her nerves, so I decided this would be a good place to escape. Elsa lasted less than an hour before she demanded to return to the palace after incessant complaining about the shortage of modern conveniences."

Kate ran her palm along the back of the brown suede sofa, stirring Marc's libido to life. "No indoor plumbing?"

Marc closed and locked the door behind him. "Not enough outlets in the bathroom for her appliances."

A smile played at the corners of her mouth. "I would think if you were here, she wouldn't need any appliances."

Her show of humor encouraged Marc somewhat. "Appliances as in hair dryers and myriad curling irons. Elsa spends hours in preparation from the minute she crawls out of bed."

Definitely the wrong thing to say, Marc realized when Kate's frown deepened. He made a mental note not to use "Elsa" and "bed" in the same sentence again. In fact, he vowed not to mention Elsa's name in any context unless absolutely necessary.

"Elsa's a real beauty queen, huh?" Kate asked wryly.

So much for that plan. "Elsa is high-maintenance. She makes a living from being—" Do not say beautiful, Marc. "From being presentable."

"Oh, I see. But I don't see how your mother could get on anyone's nerves. She's wonderful."

"Mother was not overly fond of Elsa. It was nothing like your relationship with her. I do believe she thinks you are responsible for the sunrise each morning."

"I like your mother, too, Marc. She's a great lady. And she loves you."

Sometimes Marc wondered, yet he didn't want to broach that subject now, or think about it, for that matter. "Would you like to see the rest of the place? Make certain you find it suitable for your needs?"

Kate shrugged. "I didn't bring any appliances, so I don't care about outlets. I also didn't bring any clothes and I assume that means we won't be here long."

Marc leveled his gaze on her. "You've assumed wrong. I plan to keep you here through the night, and you will not need any clothes."

She brushed her hair away from her face and tipped up her chin in defiance. "You are a very confident king."

"Only determined, Kate."

"Determined to do what?"

"To spend quality time with you. To make up for my disregard over the past few days. I've missed you."

She walked to the large window that faced the forest behind the cabin and pulled back the curtain, keeping her back to him. "I've missed you, too, but that doesn't mean I'm quite ready to forgive you for ignoring me for the past week."

Marc came up behind her and took a chance by circling his arms around her waist. "I will attempt to earn your forgiveness and alleviate your anger tonight."

When she started to turn, he commanded, "Don't."

"Why not?"

"I have something for you." He withdrew the necklace from his pocket and told her, "Hold up your hair." When she submitted, he kissed her neck and then clasped the chain, before taking her by the shoulders and turning her around. The delicate emerald necklace, surrounded by diamonds, rested between her breasts. Marc traced the oval with a fingertip. "As I predicted, it matches your eyes."

Kate lifted the stone and studied it with awe. "Oh, Marc, it's beautiful."

"And so are you."

He saw a glimpse of gratitude and pure pleasure in her gaze. He planned to see more of that tonight, especially the pleasure. "Why did you do this?" she asked.

"Let's just say it is a token of my appreciation, a peace offering of sorts. I know it's probably an inadequate gesture but—"

She placed a fingertip to his lips. "It's wonderful. No one's ever given me such an incredible gift."

Marc realized Kate had given much more than he'd warranted. "You deserve the best, Kate. I only wish my current problems did not involve you."

"Why don't we just forget about everything tonight? Let's just be together and not think about anything else."

"A very good idea. Then you forgive me?"

She toyed with the necklace. "I'm warming up to the idea."

He intended to do more than warm her up. He wanted to make her hot. But first things first. "Now I have something else to show you."

She sent him a sassy smile. "Is it in your pants, too?"

"I would be happy to allow you to do a full body search, but not now. What I want you to see is in another room."

He took her hand and led her into the great hall that held the massive dining-room table, now laid out with myriad canapés, cheeses, fruit, dishes and desserts for their evening meal.

Kate turned around the room and took in the various coats of arms hanging along the paneled walls and the twenty-foot, floor-to-ceiling russet stone fireplace. "This room is huge. Do you use it for entertaining dignitaries?"

Marc moved to the table and leaned against it. "Actually, I've rarely had any guests. It was originally a ski lodge and when the owners retired, I purchased the place as my own private haven." His place to escape.

Kate surveyed the banquet awaiting them. "Oh. I thought

maybe we're expecting the entire continent for dinner, considering all the food."

Marc had gone to a great deal of trouble having the meal prepared and delivered by the staff. It was excessive, but very impressive to the observer. "It's all for us."

She strolled along the table's edge, sampling a few items as she went. "I'm not sure I'm *that* hungry."

"We could wait until later, if you wish." He could think of other ways to spend the time.

She slid her fingertip through the chocolate mousse and licked it, sparking Marc's imagination. "Come to think of it, I could use some food." She claimed the high-back chair at the end of the table, farthest from the food, without taking a plate. "Okay, let's eat."

"Kate, there is no one here to serve us."

She rested her clasped hands in front of her. "You're here. If you want my forgiveness, then you're going to have to work for it."

Marc saw no problem with that. He predicted finding many ways to make it up to her with lovemaking she would not soon forget. Nor would he.

He took a plate and heaped it full of the fare, carefully selecting several baked oysters still housed in their shells. He had never proven or disproven their aphrodisiac qualities, but he assumed it could not hurt.

After filling his own plate and pouring two glasses of wine, he took the chair on the side of the table closest to her, expecting her to begin eating. Instead, she simply stared at him.

"Do you not find my choices satisfactory?" he asked.

"I'd like it better if you fed me."

Fed her? Kate, the confident doctor who had made it quite clear she disdained being helpless? Yet when he noted the fiery look in her eyes, he realized this could be her idea of foreplay. Obviously, he was losing his insight into the feminine mind. He would make it up to her with his knowledge of the feminine body.

He started with the oysters first, holding the fork to her lips and frankly expecting her to protest. Instead, she took the bite without any revulsion, a point in her favor. Many did not enjoy the delicacy as he did.

"I love these," she said after swallowing the bite.

"So do I." And he loved the way her lips looked at the moment, moist and pursed with pleasure. "What shall it be now?"

She nodded toward the fruit. "Grapes. I've always wanted someone to feed me grapes."

He complied, popping the fruit into her mouth. She chewed slowly, deliberately. And when she streaked her tongue across her bottom lip, Marc's jeans grew unbearably tight.

He picked up the glass of wine and offered it to her. "Would you care for something to drink now?"

She nodded and he held the glass to her lips and in his haste, inadvertently tipped it too far and missed the mark. The liquid ran down her chin and onto the front of her pale pink T-shirt. When he muttered an apology and reached for a napkin, she said, "Don't use that."

He dropped the napkin and locked into her gaze. "What would you wish me to use?"

"Your imagination, and if that doesn't work, your mouth will do."

Marc decided he could quite possibly lift the table with the strength of his erection when Kate crossed her arms over her chest then pulled her T-shirt over head, leaving her clad in only a white lace bra and jeans.

He stood, leaned over the table then slowly licked the scarlet path down her chin, her throat and on to the cleft of her breasts where he paused to outline the necklace with one fingertip. All the while, Kate kept her hands braced on the arms of the chair as if she might slide away. Marc would definitely not have that.

Once he was through with his thorough cleaning and re-settled into his chair, he expected Kate to suggest they forgo the meal and go to the bedroom. Instead, she rose, turned her back to the table and scooted onto the cloth-covered surface, leaning back until she was laid out before Marc like a center-fold. She rolled to her side and faced him, her bent arm and palm providing support for her cheek.

She nodded toward the trays. "You know, that quiche looked really good."

Marc wasn't too sure he could find the strength to leave her to get the damn quiche, considering the picture she now presented and his supreme state of arousal. But he forced himself to move back to the end of the table to retrieve a slice of the pie.

He came back to her and offered a heaping forkful. She wagged a finger at him. "This isn't for me, it's for you. Un-less, of course, you believe that old adage that real men don't eat quiche."

"Real men are up for any challenge." He was definitely up for it.

She sat up and released her bra, tossed it aside then dipped her finger in the filling to paint a design around and between her breasts.

Truthfully, Marc didn't care for the dish, but he would put aside his tastes for a taste of this woman who surprised him at every turn. After Kate lay back, he had no trouble remov-ing the quiche trail with his mouth, pausing to sample her nip-ples that peaked to perfection as he suckled them with a slow pull of his lips. He continued his course down her torso, think-ing the very best was yet to come.

When he stood and walked to the end of the table, Kate braced on her elbows and stared at him with dismay. "Is the party over?"

"It's only beginning. Sit up."

She did as he asked and he tugged her legs forward so he could reach the buttons on her jeans. He released them then pulled the denim down her legs until she was left wearing only white lace panties and a devilish smile.

"I personally favor the chocolate mousse," he said.

She swallowed hard. "I agree. It's very good."

"And I will endeavor to be very good, too, Kate." He went back to the spread of food and picked up the entire bowl of dessert. When he came back to Kate, he swirled his finger in the mousse then held it to her lips. She took his finger into her mouth and withdrew it slowly with an added flick of her tongue across the tip.

It was all Marc could do not to throw the bowl across the room and take her right there. Instead, he moved back to the end of the table and painted the inside of her legs with the chocolate dessert. He definitely preferred this to the quiche and after placing the bowl on the chair, he went to work enjoying every last bite.

He started at Kate's ankle, working his way up to her knee then on to the crease of her thigh. He moved to her other leg and did the same until all the dessert had disappeared.

He straightened to find Kate watching him, her breasts rising and falling with every ragged breath, her eyes clouded with need.

"What would you like me to sample now, Kate?"

"Anything that suits your fancy."

He took her hands and pulled her forward until her legs dangled completely over the edge of the table. "Anything?"

She sighed. "Anything."

He slid her panties away. "Are you certain?"

"Yes."

He started with her mouth, sweeping his tongue inside to savor the piquant taste of wine and the sweet taste of Kate. He moved to her breasts, feasting on one, then the other, while Kate firmly planted her hands on his head, following his movements. He ended by taking a seat in the chair Kate had occupied and centering his attention on the soft shading between her thighs, first testing the territory with his fingertips, then with his mouth. He had imagined doing this to her, only to hold back until he thought the time was right. The time was definitely right.

Kate thought she might totally fade away into a carnal void, or bolt off the table at the first sweep of Marc's tongue. She thought she might demand that he stop because it was almost too much to bear, the intensity of the sensations as he explored her with more finesse that she'd ever thought possible. She thought she might actually scream when he slipped a finger inside her, then two, while he continued working his magic with his incredible mouth.

This kind of intimacy made her feel so open, so vulnerable, yet in some ways so free. She simply gave in to the moment, gave herself over to the feelings, the building pleasure facilitated by Marc, who knew exactly what he was doing—and what he was doing to her. He was completely possessing her, and she willingly relinquished all control. She had no choice.

The orgasm hit her fast and furiously, sapping her strength, causing her to bow over and rest her head against Marc's. Never before had she reacted so strongly to a climax. Completely and utterly lost, she rode the waves of pleasure, her whole body trembling with the force of the release, until reality broke through the bliss.

This wild, decadent behavior was so out of character for normally cautious Kate, something she had dared to imagine only in her most secret fantasies. Now Marc DeLoria had brought those fantasies to life, and with that came a few revelations.

She understood all too well why women were drawn to him. He was the ultimate lover. But what she loved about

Marc went far beyond his sensual skills. She loved the man who resided beneath the exterior. She loved him with all of her heart and she would always love him, even if he didn't have a penny to his name or a place in a monarchy. Even if he never loved her.

Kate couldn't control the sob that escaped her mouth or the ensuing tears that she'd never wanted him to see. But he did see them as he raised his head, confusion and concern calling out from his endless dark blue eyes. Now she was totally open, body and soul, and she hated being that exposed.

He stood, wrapped his arms around her and held her for several moments until she regained some of her composure. Then he lifted her chin and thumbed away a tear.

"Kate," he said softly. "Did I hurt you?"

She shook her head. "No, not at all."

"Then what's wrong?"

"I don't know."

He brushed a kiss across her forehead and framed her face in his palms. "There is no shame in what we've done."

"I'm not ashamed," she said, followed by a sniff. "I'm just surprised by my behavior. I've never done anything like this before."

"Do you not think that I know that?"

"I don't know what you think. You're hard to read."

He sighed. "I care a great deal about you, Kate. I only want to give you pleasure and make you feel as good as you make me feel when I'm with you."

He *only* wanted to give her pleasure. She'd known this all along, his resistance to commitment. But it didn't make it any easier for Kate to accept. Regardless, she would take what time they had together and keep it close to her heart and her own feelings close to the vest. "I'm just a little overwhelmed."

"Are you certain that's all it is? You're not usually one to hide your feelings."

If he knew what she was hiding—that she was in love with him—he would have to make a retraction and probably run like the wind. "I'm okay now. Really."

"Do you want me to take you back to the palace?"

That was the last thing Kate wanted. These moments with Marc might never come again, and she intended to enjoy each one. "Actually, I want you to take me to bed and ravish me."

"You're positive that's what you want?"

She grinned despite the ache in her heart. "If you think you're man enough."

By the time Marc carried Kate into his bedroom, he wasn't certain he was man enough to give her everything she needed beyond the physical aspects. Her tears had taken him by surprise, caused him to assess where their relationship was leading. Yet with her standing before him bathed in firelight coming from the corner hearth, beautifully naked, he could not think beyond the moment, or consider anything but this time they had now.

He led her to the bed and nudged her onto the edge, then undressed while she watched. As ready as he was to make love to her, he thought it might be best to simply hold her for a time.

He tossed aside the covers and told her, "Climb in."

She did as he asked and he walked to the opposite side of the bed, then slid between the sheets. Kate settled her head against his shoulder and slid her fingers through the hair on his chest. She paused to stroke his nipples, then moved on to his abdomen, circling her finger in his navel.

This wouldn't do, Marc decided. Not if he wanted prove to her—and to himself—that he could be in bed with a woman without the sole intent of bedding a woman. "Turn to your side, away from me."

She raised her head, her hand poised immediately above dangerous ground. "What?"

"Right now I only want to hold you."

"Hold me?

"Yes. Is there something wrong with that?"

"No, not if that's what you really want." Her voice sounded tentative.

He brushed a kiss over her lips, keeping it chaste in order to keep his desire in check. "For now, that is what I really want."

She rolled to her side and he fitted himself to her back, gritting his teeth when she nestled her bottom against him. He draped one arm over her hip then slipped the other beneath his pillow, contacting the condom he'd put there in preparation for this moment. He drew back his hand as if he'd been bit.

"Are you comfortable?" he asked, his cheek resting against hers.

"I'm fine, Marc. You don't have to do this."

"I want to do this." And he did, more than he had realized to this point.

Tonight marked a milestone for Marc DeLoria. He had an incredible, sensual woman in his arms. A woman he wanted so much that he physically hurt from the intensity of his need. Yet he found a certain satisfaction in knowing he was stronger than he'd assumed, than anyone had assumed. And he had Kate to thank for that.

He wanted to tell her again how much she meant to him, this time with more conviction than before. But truthfully, he was almost afraid to tell her, for fear he might be forced to admit to himself that he was that defenseless.

Instead, he held her tighter and simply enjoyed the placid atmosphere—the fragrant floral scent of Kate's hair, the crackling logs in the fireplace, the cool breeze filtering in from the partially open window at his back.

Just when he felt his body starting to calm, Kate reached back and ran her palm down his hip and his thigh, then back up again. And when she rubbed her bottom against him, he again grew hard as granite. She turned her face toward him and Marc responded by kissing her. A long, deep kiss resurrecting the desire he had for Kate, crushing his determination to only hold her.

With his last ounce of strength, he broke the kiss and buried his face in her hair. "Kate, we—"

"Need to be closer," she said on a broken breath, then rolled onto her back. "I need to be close to you. I want you inside me."

Marc gave up his resistance, grabbed the condom from beneath his pillow and tore it open. He had it in place in a matter of moments and rose above Kate. When he guided himself inside her, he was overcome with the feeling of completion. He had insulated himself against this very thing for most of his life, and he wasn't prepared for what he felt at that moment.

He reined in those foreign emotions and kissed her again, holding her closely with his hands beneath her bottom, bringing her up to meet his thrusts.

Sheer pleasure, he thought. Mind-shattering, incredible pleasure.

"You feel so good," Kate whispered between kisses. "I can't believe how good."

"So do you, *mon amour,*" he whispered.

My love. He had called her his love.

Marc was shaken to the core. He'd learned at a relatively early age how to please a woman, but he'd never resorted to professing love in the heat of the moment. Was this only the heat of the moment, or blind truth staring him in the face?

Kate's eyes reflected the glow of the firelight, and he saw something there that went beyond physical need. Perhaps she expected more declarations, more than he could give her.

With effort, he slipped from Kate's body, wanting it to last, to make it a memorable experience for Kate, or so he told himself, when he knew deep down that he was pulling away from the intimacy.

His actions immediately brought about Kate's protest. "Where are you going?"

"I'm going to make this better for you. For us."

She frowned. "I'm not sure I can stand much better."

"Roll back to your side, and trust me."

Kate did as he'd requested, and Marc once more fitted himself against her back, slid his arms around her and pulled her closer.

"Oh, yes," Kate murmured as he slipped into her welcoming heat again.

He caressed her breasts with one hand and divined the damp, smooth flesh between her thighs with the other, plying her with long, fluid strokes as he moved within her, with her. Marc slowed the pace to regain his bearings. He'd mistakenly believed that by not looking into her eyes, he could distance himself. Instead, he only felt closer to her, totally one with her. Maybe it was time he stop fighting this, fighting her. Fighting himself and his feelings.

Kate's body went rigid in his arms, but it wasn't from fulfillment, that much Marc realized when she abruptly raised her head. "Do you hear that?"

He couldn't hear much of anything aside from the pulse pounding in his ears. "Hear what?"

"Footsteps."

Marc clenched his jaw and stopped all motion to listen. "I imagine it's only the caretakers," he said, even though talking took great effort. "They've come to put away the food."

"Are you sure?" She sounded wary, something Marc decided to remedy by resuming his touch, more deliberately this time, until he felt her relax somewhat.

"Don't worry," he whispered. "They won't bother us."

Marc ran his tongue along the shell of Kate's ear and picked up the tempo of his thrusts. Then he discerned footfalls coming down the corridor, louder this time.

"They're…getting…closer," Kate said, but continued to be an active participant in their lovemaking, belying any real concern.

"They will not come in here," Marc assured her, although he briefly wondered why the caretaker or his wife would be seeking him out after he'd left instructions, in no uncertain terms, not to be disturbed.

"But what if…" She drew in a ragged breath. "What if they do come in?"

Right now Marc did not give a damn if every member of the council paid them a visit. He was on the verge of a searing climax, and so, he suspected, was Kate. "Let them, dammit. I can't stop."

The footsteps grew heavier, louder as Marc moved harder and deeper within Kate. The minute the rap came at the door, the orgasm claimed Kate and she cried out, in turn, bringing about Marc's own climax.

Marc drifted back to coherency, enough to realize another knock had sounded at the door, his euphoria now replaced by frustration and anger.

"Shouldn't you answer?" Kate whispered. "Someone might need you."

Someone's head was going to roll. "Not yet." He did not want to let her go. The knock was more insistent this time, very close to pounding.

Marc shouted, "What do you want!"

A long moment of silence passed before the offending party said, "I am sorry to disturb you, Your Elusiveness, but I must speak with you."

Nicholas.

What in the hell was he doing here?

Obviously bent on losing his job, Marc thought. Unless there was some dire emergency. That brought Marc to his senses and sent him away from Kate to gather his robe from the end of the four-poster bed. He discarded the condom, shrugged on the robe and stalked to the door, tempted to throw it open from the force of his fury over the interference. Realizing Kate was still in his bed, naked, he opened the door only wide enough to confront his attendant.

"This better be good," Marc said, not bothering to hide his irritation.

"My apologies for the intrusion, Your Virileness."

Marc gritted his teeth and spoke through them. "Just spit it out, Nicholas."

"The queen mother has asked me to summon you. It seems that our youngest guest will not go to sleep without Dr. Milner's assistance. The household is at its wit's end. I would have called, but you left your phone behind."

Marc regretted leaving behind information on where he and Kate would be. "For God's sake, Cecile is an infant. Getting her to sleep is not that difficult. Tell my mother to have Beatrice practice more persistence."

"It's okay, Marc."

Marc turned to find Kate clutching the sheet to her neck. "Cecile's still trying to adjust," she said. "I don't mind seeing about her."

Marc minded, and he was bloody well having a difficult time adjusting to the thought that his night with Kate had come to an abrupt halt. "We will be returning within the hour. In the meantime, tell my mother she owes Dr. Milner a huge debt, and myself as well."

Nicholas nodded. "I will pass on that message, and again my apologies for the interruption."

Nicholas walked away, muttering under his breath. Marc couldn't really blame the man. After all, he hadn't come here to retrieve them of his own volition.

Making his way back to the bed, Marc snapped on the floor lamp and sat on the edge of the mattress. Kate stared up at him, regret etched in her expression. Marc could certainly relate.

He brushed her hair away from her forehead and planted a kiss where the faint bruise now resided. "Will she ever sleep through the night?"

"Yes, she will, as soon as she learns to go back to sleep on her own. She won't do that unless you stop your little midnight visits."

Hell, he'd been caught. "How would you know about that?"

She raised his hand to her lips and kissed his palm. "Because I've been sleeping the past few nights in the room next to the nursery. I don't return to the guesthouse until a couple of hours before dawn when Beatrice relieves me."

"I thought I was doing the right thing."

She held his hand against her warm cheek. "I think you're doing a wonderful job, although you might want to reconsider so she will learn to get herself back to sleep."

"I admit it. I've grown soft. I cannot stand to see her cry." He kissed her gently. "I cannot stand to see any woman cry, especially if I am the reason for her tears."

Kate smiled. "I promise you, a few minutes ago, I wasn't crying."

He returned her smile. "I know. You were moaning."

Her eyes widened. "Was I?"

"Yes, you were, and quite sufficiently. So was I."

"Do you think Nicholas heard us?"

"If not the moans, then he probably heard the headboard hitting the wall."

"We did that?"

"Yes, we did."

Kate covered her face with her hands. "I won't be able to face him now."

Marc took advantage of Kate's release of the sheet and lowered it, revealing her bare breasts. He played his thumb back and forth over one nipple. "I had hoped to make more noise throughout the night."

Kate dropped her hands from her face and sighed. "Me, too. I still haven't seen the royal birthmark."

Grinning, Marc stood, turned his back on Kate and lowered the robe to immediately below his waist.

"Wow. It looks like an inverted ice cream cone."

First, he felt Kate's fingertips outlining the birthmark above his right buttock, then the play of her warm lips against his flesh. That was all it took to convince Marc that he could not take Kate anywhere at the moment except back to bed.

When he turned and dropped the robe to the floor, Kate's lips parted in surprise. "I thought we were leaving, Marc."

"Not yet." He climbed back in beside Kate and hovered over her. "Cecile is relatively cheerful this time of night. My mother and Beatrice can entertain her while I finish entertaining you."

"Marc, she's going to know what took us so long."

"And your point?"

"I don't want to her to think—"

"That we are engaging in very hot and very hard…" He pressed against her, letting her know it would not be long before he recovered. "Lovemaking?"

"Well, since you put it that way."

He winked. "I am going to put it another way. Kate, I do not care what my mother thinks we are doing. I only care about doing it, and I promise you that's exactly what I intend to do."

With that, he slid down Kate's body, leaving wet kisses in his path, determined to show Kate that he was a man of his word.

Nine

Together Kate and Marc put Cecile back to sleep, just like a real family. But Kate acknowledged that the concept was only an illusion, even after their evening together. And she had to decide how much more she could take before she lost herself to him completely, although she was probably already too late.

Standing outside the nursery, Marc pulled her into his arms and murmured, "Come to my bed with me."

Kate would like nothing better, but every time he kissed her, made love to her, he stole another chunk of her heart. "I think I should just go back to the guesthouse. Otherwise, we'll never get any sleep."

Marc dropped his arms from around her and shoved his hands into his pockets. "I suppose you're right. We wouldn't want the staff to start making assumptions. That would only serve to make matters worse."

Kate was hoping Marc might put up a little more of a fight. But once again, his reputation and rumors prevented them from having their relationship out in the open. "First, I need to tell you what Beatrice told me today."

"You spoke with her? Why did you wait until now to tell me?"

"I think it's because you've kept my mouth occupied most of the night."

Marc released a gruff sigh. "If you continue to make those comments, then I'll say to hell with the staff and carry you to my bed."

"Promises, promises."

He looked mock-serious. "Kate, I'm warning you."

And she'd learned to heed those warnings that afternoon. "Okay, okay. Back to Beatrice."

Kate wasn't sure how to proceed except to be blunt and hope Marc took the news well. "Basically, she said that she heard your brother did have a lover aside from the countess. She saw them together at the guesthouse one night while she was walking in the gardens. But she couldn't give me a name or any description."

Marc didn't look pleased, but at least he didn't look angry. "That's not much to go on, but it's a start."

"Yeah, I guess it is, although I'm not very optimistic we'll find out much more any time soon."

"We have to keep trying. I have to know for certain if Cecile is Philippe's child, then decide how much information I'm willing to release. Regardless, at some point in time, we will have to reveal Cecile is not your child, or mine."

Kate sighed. "You know, I'm really too tired to even think about it now. I just wish I could go to bed and wake up to find this whole rumor mess is nothing more than a nightmare."

Marc's expression turned all too serious. "This is beginning to take its toll on you, isn't it?"

"I'll survive."

"I'm certain you will, but you have to realize that it could get much worse before it ends."

"How so?"

"You could be shunned at the clinic. Patients could refuse to see you if they begin to believe the rumors."

"If it happens, I'll just ignore it."

"It will not be that easy to ignore if it does happen, and you might have to make some choices in terms of your career."

Had she not been a knowledgeable doctor, Kate would have sworn her heart just stopped. "What are you saying?"

"I'm saying that you might consider returning to the States, at least until this is all cleared up."

"Is that what you want me to do?"

"This isn't about what I want. It's about protecting you from the brutality that I've experienced my entire life. It's not an easy thing to deal with."

Until that point, Kate had been prepared to deal with it. Now, she wasn't so sure. Marc was telling her that he believed it would be best for her to go home. Maybe he was right. Maybe she should walk out of his life. Maybe that's exactly what he intended to do, provide her with an easy out.

"I'll seriously consider what you're saying," she said, trying to keep a tight hold on her anger and hurt, "and I think you could be right. If I'm not around, then that would at least end the rumors of our clandestine affair that just happens to really be taking place."

"Kate, I want you to be—"

"I know, Marc. You want me to be careful. You want me to be safe. And I want…" *You to love me.* "I want to go to bed, alone, so I can finally get a good night's sleep."

She turned to leave before the annoying tears paid her another visit.

"I'll be by to see you in the morning, Kate."

Kate stopped in the hall and without turning around said, "I'd prefer to be by myself tomorrow."

She hurried away, yet still hoped that maybe Marc would

call her back and tell her he didn't want her to leave, that he wanted her to stay for good.

It didn't happen.

But what could she expect? Marc DeLoria was a good-time guy who had enough to worry about besides Kate Milner. And obviously she'd misunderstood when he'd said "My love" when they'd made love earlier. Maybe he'd meant nothing by it. Maybe he'd said that to many more women.

But Kate wasn't competing with a woman; she was competing with a kingdom. And she would do well to remember that from now on, even if she would never forget the time they'd spent together—or him.

On Sunday, Marc granted Kate's wish and left her alone. Even when she went to the palace to help tend to Cecile and then dined with Mary, she didn't see him. Again, he had totally withdrawn from life—her life. But then, she had told him she'd wanted to be by herself. In reality, she'd hoped he would have ignored her request. Instead, he'd totally ignored her, period.

By Monday morning, Kate regretted that she hadn't sought him out and insisted they talk one more time, and she regretted that she hadn't just laid it on the line and told him she was in love with him. At least then she would have lessened some of the burden. But she felt the full weight of the decisions she would have to make when she entered the clinic, a place where she had found satisfaction in doing what she did best—treating people who truly appreciated her efforts.

Kate had opted to come in early to complete the paperwork she'd left last Friday. She wouldn't want to leave any unfinished business in case she did decide to return home. And that included unfinished business with Marc. But that would have to come later, if she could ever get him alone again.

As she passed through the corridor, the sound of heated voices coming from Renault's office halted her progress. She stopped to listen, realizing that the devious doctor had obviously ignored Marc's dismissal. She also recognized a woman's voice, at first believing it to be Isabella, the lustful nurse. She was very much Renault's type. But when the woman spoke again, Kate was shocked to realize it was Caroline, her linguistic aide and clinic champion.

Although it went against her grain to eavesdrop, Kate remained outside the door to listen, shock holding her in place when she heard Caroline say, "I have done what you've asked of me. I delivered the baby to the palace with the note. I will not do any more, Jonathan."

"The king is forcing me to leave my job. I will not stop until I ruin him."

"Well, you'll have to ruin him all by yourself."

"Then it is over between us," Renault hissed.

"This will be no hardship for me, I assure you," Caroline said.

Kate wasn't surprised that Renault had set his sights on the blond-haired, brown-eyed beauty, but she was surprised that Caroline had succumbed to his suspect charms. Still, she wanted to cheer, both from Caroline's insult and the knowledge she had gained about Cecile's mysterious arrival at the palace. Then she wanted to shriek when the door flew open and Renault stormed out. He shoved her arm on his way down the hall, sending her a look of disdain over one shoulder as he tore through the doors leading to the waiting room.

"Good riddance," Kate muttered as Caroline joined her in the hallway.

The nurse placed a shaky hand to her throat as if she feared someone might strangle her. "Dr. Milner, I didn't know you had come in."

"Well, I'm here, and we need to talk." She gestured toward the office Caroline had just left. "In here."

When they both entered, Kate shut the door and faced Caroline, who looked as though she might faint. "I overheard your conversation with Dr. Renault."

"All of it?"

"Enough to know that you're the one who left little Cecile at the palace gates. Are you her mother?"

Caroline shook her head and her eyes filled with tears. "No, but I did raise her from the time she was born."

"Then you know the identity of her mother."

She looked away. "Yes. She was my best friend."

Was? "Where is she now?"

Caroline sniffed. "She died after giving birth to Cecile."

Kate experienced a twinge of sympathy. "Why haven't you come forward with this information?"

"I promised I wouldn't say anything."

"Who did you promise?"

"Jonathan."

Kate's sympathy went the way of the wind. "That creep? He has no right to ask that of you. Why would you get involved with him?"

Caroline withdrew a tissue from her pocket and blew her nose. "He threatened me, told me that he would have me fired from my job if I didn't do as he asked. He can be very convincing."

Not as far as Kate was concerned. "Why did you tell him in the first place?"

"Because we were lovers. Because I thought I could trust him when I decided I needed to come forward. He was the one who came up with the plan to leave Cecile at the palace with the anonymous note indicating she was a DeLoria. In order to protect me, or so he said, since it took me so long to make the decision. It turns out that Jonathan saw this as a way to exact revenge after King Marcel threatened to fire him because of staff complaints. He's very envious of Marcel DeLoria. He despises him."

That much Kate already knew. "Now let me get this

straight. He convinced you to give the baby away and leave a note that claimed she's a DeLoria?"

Caroline raised her red-rimmed eyes to Kate. "She is a DeLoria, Dr. Milner."

"Then one of the DeLoria sons is her father?"

"Yes."

Drawing in a breath, Kate prepared to ask the question she would rather avoid, but she had to know. "Which son?"

"King Philippe."

Kate wanted to collapse from relief. "Your friend and Philippe were lovers?"

"They were more than that, Dr. Milner. They were married. No one knew because King Philippe believed the country could not accept Lisette. She was a commoner. She worked at the tailor's in St. Simone. That's how they met. They loved each other very much, but they had to keep it hidden from the world."

Kate took a moment to let the information sink in before she said, "But Philippe was engaged to a countess."

"Yes, and that was a front. Countess Trudeau knew all along about the marriage and agreed to pose as his fiancée, at least until King Philippe decided how to break the news to his family that he planned to abdicate the throne to his brother. He wanted to be with Lisette and raise their child together, whether anyone accepted her or not. That was the reason for the countess's and the king's two-year engagement, and the reason why the countess married so soon after King Philippe's death."

Kate sighed. "He was willing to give it all up for the woman he loved."

"Yes, but before he could, it was too late. He never had the opportunity to tell anyone." A tear escaped and rolled down Caroline's cheek. "He never saw his beautiful baby girl."

The tragedy was beginning to unfold, piece by piece, and

it was all Kate could do not to cry a few of her own tears. "Were you there with Lisette when she gave birth?"

"Yes. I tried to save her, I swear it. But when I realized I needed help, I called the king. He had just returned from Paris and he was on his way to take Lisette to the hospital when he lost control of the car."

"And Lisette—"

"Died only hours after Cecile was born. She made me promise to help Philippe take care of little Cecile and to tell him that she would always love him. I never had the chance, but I did take care of the baby and loved her the best way I knew how, and I do love her still. But I've always believed she belongs to her rightful family. I just didn't know what to do, since no one knew about Lisette and Philippe."

Even though her evasiveness had threatened Marc's standing with his people, Kate very much understood the woman's dilemma. "Caroline, I'm so sorry you got caught up in this mess, but you did take care of Cecile very well. She's happy and healthy. The family owes you a great deal for that."

Caroline's tears came full force now. "I will tell King Marcel the details if you wish me to. And I am prepared to suffer the consequences of my deception."

Kate recognized that the nurse's only real mistake had been her involvement with the devil doctor, Renault. "I'm sure the royal family will understand that you were put in a very precarious position and will choose to be lenient. They may not be so kind to Jonathan Renault."

Anger turned Caroline's eyes a deeper brown. "He deserves the harshest punishment. He is responsible for the rumors and the attempts at discrediting the king. And you."

"Well, at least we can clear everything up now with King Marcel."

Caroline stuffed the weathered tissue back into her pocket.

"I will gather my things and leave today. The clinic has the number where I can be reached."

"You can't quit, Caroline."

"But I assumed—"

"That you would lose your job? Not if I can prevent it. You're a wonderful nurse. The clinic needs you. I do, too." Kate smiled. "How else am I going to be able to tell the difference between a sore throat and a sore back?"

Caroline hugged Kate for a few moments, then drew back with a joyful expression. "My sincerest gratitude, Dr. Milner. The clinic most definitely needs you, too. The patients are much more fond of you than they ever were of Jonathan. Many of them have refused to see him since your arrival."

That concept gave Kate pause. The patients did need her, and if she left now, she would be leaving them in a lurch. She would definitely need to stay, at least until a suitable replacement was found, or if Marc tried to change her mind about going home.

Marc.

She had to call him immediately and tell him the puzzle was finally solved. Now if she could just put the pieces of her heart back together if he didn't ask her to stay.

Marc hadn't waited long enough for them to bring round the car before he'd climbed inside the Corvette and taken the hairpin mountain curves at excessive speeds, leaving behind the armored car full of guards as well as his mother, who waited back at the palace for word. He'd reached the hospital in record time, forced into action by Kate's phone call stating she had solved the mystery of Cecile's parentage. Now he sprinted down the hospital corridor toward Kate's office and burst inside, startling Kate, who sat at her desk, looking very unnerved.

"Tell me now," he demanded. "Is Cecile Philippe's child?"

Kate rose, rounded the desk and perched on the edge. "Yes, she is your brother's child."

Hearing the confirmation sent shock spiraling through Marc. "And the mother?"

"She was a commoner, a tailor's assistant."

"Where is she?"

Kate's gaze faltered. "She's dead, Marc. She died following Cecile's birth, the same night Philippe died trying to reach her to bring her back here."

Marc streaked a hand over his forehead, now covered in beads of sweat, both from his harried departure and the unfathomable information. "Then he did have a lover other than the countess."

"No, Marc, she wasn't his lover. She was his wife. And he was about to abdicate the throne to you so that they could be together."

And Marc had thought he couldn't suffer more shock. "No one knew?"

"Only Caroline, the nurse I've been working with. She was Cecile's mother's friend and she raised the baby until she returned her to the palace. Jonathan Renault was also involved, with Caroline and with the worst of the schemes."

"He was behind this after all?"

"Yes, and there's more."

Kate recounted what she'd learned earlier about Philippe and the woman named Lisette, the nurse and her connection with Renault, and Renault's plans to destroy Marc. When she was finished, she said, "Now that everything is cleared up, I'm asking that you not be too hard on Caroline. She's a good employee and she didn't ask for any of this. She's been a victim of Renault's deceit and had it not been for her, who knows what would have become of Cecile?"

Caroline remaining as an employee of the clinic was the least of Marc's concerns. "I will see to it she keeps her job. But

I have no recourse other than to have Renault arrested for treason."

"He's on his way to Paris," Kate said. "I spoke with his landlord, who informed me he'd gotten in his car about an hour ago and taken off. Or at least I think that's what he said. His English wasn't too good, and we know my French isn't too great."

"You talked to him by phone?"

"In person."

"You went to Renault's house to confront him? That was dangerous, Kate."

She smiled. "Believe me, I wasn't worried. I planned to tell him you were on your way. If that didn't work, a swift kick would have."

Marc was too uptight to smile, too wound up to find any humor in the situation. "That was unwise, Kate, a huge risk."

She shrugged. "Well, I said I wanted some adventure, and this has been quite an adventure."

Marc didn't like the way she'd said that, as if the adventure was over. "At least now you can go back to your duties here without worrying about the press or Renault."

She studied her hands clasped tightly in her lap. "Marc, I've decided to stay here only until you find someone to replace me. You were probably right about me returning to the States. Maybe that would be best for everyone, especially you."

Marc fought an unfamiliar panic. "You have no reason to leave now, Kate. Everyone will know that you are not Cecile's mother." He sounded almost desperate, probably because he was.

She glanced up at him. "*If* you decide to reveal the truth, and I'm not sure you would want to do that if you consider what it might mean to Philippe's reputation."

Marc wondered if the truth would damage Philippe's reputation if everyone knew the whole story, that his love for a woman had driven him to deceive his people. But would his mother be receptive to telling all? He wasn't certain he would be willing to take the chance if it meant destroying his brother's memory. As much as he'd despised trying to live up to Philippe's example, he wanted his brother to be remembered for the great man he had been—a man who had been willing to give up his title for the sake of love.

That concept was as unfamiliar to Marc as driving the speed limit on rural roads. Or it had been before he'd met Kate.

He didn't want her to leave, yet he could not hold her against her will. "If you want to return to the States, that's your decision. But I would like for you to stay."

"Why, Marc?"

"You're very much needed here at the hospital."

"Is that the only reason?"

"Cecile needs you, too." *Just say it, dammit.* "And I—"

The loud knock at the door cut off Marc's declaration and provoked a foul curse bursting forth from his mouth before he could stop it. He threw open the door, again finding Nicholas there. The man had seriously bad timing.

"Beg pardon, Your…Majesty, but your mother insists you return to the palace immediately. It seems the media are calling for a statement from you in regard to charges leveled by a Dr. Renault, who says you've threatened to kill him, which is why he has fled the country."

"That bastard," Marc snapped. He turned to Kate, recognizing that now was not the time to make any confessions. "Kate, I have to—"

She flipped her hand toward the door. "Go on. I have a few patients to see anyway."

"I'll speak with you as soon as I have the time."

"Guess I'll see you in about a month, then." She smiled, but not before he saw the disappointment in her eyes.

"We'll talk about this later. I promise." If only he could promise her more.

Marc left her then, hating that he had caused her more pain. Hating himself because he had been such a coward. He'd had the prime opportunity to tell her that he needed her and that he cared for her more than he could express, but he'd blown it—with some help from his attendant.

Once more, duty had intruded on his private life, and that caused Marc to consider several things. Would she be willing to give up much of her privacy to be by his side? Would he be selfish to ask that of her?

Unlike Philippe, he had no one to replace him should he decide to give up the crown for love. But he didn't know if he could live with the decision to give up Kate.

Ten

"**S**o that's it, Mother. The whole story of how Cecile came to be."

In the library, Marc sat on the settee across from Mary, awaiting her reaction and finding it odd that she seemed so calm. He, on the other hand, felt as if someone were banging a drum in his head and lighting a torch to his gut.

"I suppose I didn't know Philippe as well as I thought," she said. "And I'm sad that he didn't believe he could come to me. I would have understood if he'd fallen in love."

"You might have, Mother. But the country as whole might not have accepted his choice."

Mary toyed with the bracelet at her wrist, turning it round and round. "The country is more accepting than most people realize. They accepted me when your father brought me here."

"Perhaps that's because you have more charm that most women. And you aren't exactly a commoner."

"They recognized that I loved your father greatly, and two people in love are a wonder to behold."

"How is that possible when you knew each other so briefly?"

"I knew it the moment I laid eyes on him, and he felt the same. It's not so very difficult to understand once you have been in that position."

Marc actually did understand. But he didn't have time to consider love at the moment—his love for Kate—even though he needed to think about it, and soon. Before Kate left him. "I have to decide how to handle this whole media fiasco. The people are demanding answers from me."

Mary sighed. "Those answers call for serious deliberation, especially Renault's claim that you threatened to kill him. Did you threaten him?"

"It was a veiled threat, and it did not involve killing him, although that thought did cross my mind."

"I'm very surprised, Marcel. You've always been very diplomatic."

"He called Kate a whore."

"Then you should definitely do him bodily harm."

He couldn't suppress his smile, but only allowed it for a moment. "I will deal with him without resorting to violence, Mother. Renault and his ramblings are not my greatest concern. Deciding what to reveal about Cecile's parentage is."

Mary sighed. "I am proud to claim Cecile as my grandchild, but I hate that Philippe's birthright put such pressure on him, enough to cost him his life because he felt he had to deny his true love. And now I see it happening to you. At times, I wish you weren't subjected to living your life for your people."

No one wished that more than Marc at this moment. "I have no choice."

"You should have choices, Marcel, especially when it

comes to whomever you choose to love. That is a given as far as I am concerned."

Marc understood she was referring to Kate, and he wasn't ready to discuss that with her yet. "What do you think we should do about Cecile?"

"That is your decision, my son."

"I want to know what you wish me to do."

"I want you to raise Cecile as your own."

He could not consider anything else. He loved the baby as if she were his own child, and he would continue to protect her at every turn. "I had planned to raise her, regardless of the fact that she's Philippe's daughter."

"Therein lies your answer. And I wish for you the love you deserve with Kate."

He knew it would eventually come to this. "Mother, I—"

"Marc, you have never feared much in your lifetime. You were always the one climbing the tallest tree, scaling the wall surrounding the castle." She smiled. "Chasing the most unattainable women. Do not be afraid to love."

"I'm not afraid of it. I'm just not bloody good at it."

Mary's demeanor went stern in a matter of seconds, as it often had when Marc had climbed those trees and scaled those walls. "You will never know unless you try, Marcel. Kate deserves that much from you. Unless you've been trifling with her feelings. If that is the case, I will not be pleased."

Marc thought for a moment and realized he had been guilty of many things where Kate was concerned, the least of which had been his inability to express his feelings. "In some ways maybe I haven't been fair to her, but not intentionally. I've believed all along that I could not give her what she needs. A life of her own, not a life where everyone is scrutinizing her every move."

"Have you given her that choice?"

Marc looked away. "No."

"Do you love her, Marcel?"

God, he did. "Yes, Mother, I do love her." It hadn't pained him to admit it. The ceiling did not fall down around his head, and the earth below his feet did not open up and swallow him.

"And what did she say when you told her?" Mary asked.

He braced for the fallout. "I haven't told her yet."

The fallout came swift and sure. "Oh, good grief, Marcel. What are you waiting for? A royal edict?"

He'd been waiting for the right time, the right place, the right words. "It's not as if I've had nothing better to do, Mother." A very weak excuse.

"You have certainly found the time to bed her, my son."

Touché. "I do not care to discuss this with you."

Mary flipped her white lace handkerchief in his direction. "Oh, posh. I am not brainless, Marcel. I know why you took her to the cabin, and what went on there, if not before. And I assure you that Kate takes your intimacy very seriously, and I hope you do as well this time."

This time. The anger came back to Marc once more. Would he ever live down his playboy reputation? "I'm not the same man I was before, Mother. I've changed, whether you care to believe it not."

Mary joined him on the settee and rested a delicate hand on his arm. "But have you changed enough to love only one woman? Enough to be a good father and a man whom your own father would be proud of?"

He'd never loved another woman as he loved Kate. He'd never really loved any woman aside from her. "I don't know, Mother. Why don't you tell me?"

"I truly believe you have changed, *mon fiston.*"

"If that were the case, then you would stop referring to me as your little boy."

She leaned and kissed his cheek. "You will always be my

little boy, but you are a man now, and I am very, very proud of you."

Marc had waited what seemed like a lifetime to hear those words. "Thank you, Mother. I appreciate your faith in me." A faith he had seen in Kate as well. He reveled in the fact that the two women he loved the most believed in him…or at least Kate had at one time.

Mary patted his arm. "And I would be even more proud if you would do something else for me."

Now why did that not surprise him? "What would that be, Mother?"

"Make Kate your wife."

Marry Kate? Was he ready for that? "We've had too little time together to make such a monumental decision."

"You've spent enough time together to fall in love. If it happened to your father, it most likely has happened to you. After all, you are your father's son. Had I not settled him down, he probably would have been globe-trotting well into his golden years."

But Marc had no idea if Kate loved him. After all, time and again she'd said she only wanted adventure. And a few hours ago, she'd said she planned to leave him. "Kate is considering returning home to the States."

Mary looked totally taken aback. "Why did you not tell me this sooner?"

"I didn't want to upset you further. I know how much you admire her."

"And what do you plan to do to prevent this from happening?"

Marc rested his elbows on his knees and rubbed both hands down his face. "I honestly don't know. I have too much to think about now with Renault's threats and the rumors. I'm torn between duty to my country and my commitment to Kate."

"You will simply have to consider both. Life is very short, Marcel."

And Marc was very short on time. Feeling drained, he leaned back against the sofa. "What if Kate decides to leave regardless of what I tell her?"

"Then you will have to convince her to stay."

She made it sound as if that involved no more than saying, Kate, I love you, marry me, and we'll live happily ever after. "How do you propose I do that?"

She released a mirthless laugh. "Marcel, you've spent your life wooing women. You are a highly intelligent man. I have no doubt you will find a way."

"I hope your belief in me is warranted." He hoped Kate's belief in him still existed.

"I have all the confidence in the world in you. And I assume you've decided to take my advice?"

He smiled reluctantly. "I will follow your advice and try to win Kate's heart."

"You have her heart, Marcel. Now all you have to do is come up with a plan to win her hand."

A sudden bout of determination sent Marc abruptly to his feet. "I will get on that immediately. And we'll hope that Kate hasn't left for Paris to catch the next plane out of Europe."

"I doubt she has, dear. If I know her, she's probably coming up with some way to convince you that love isn't really a four-letter word."

"And I hope I am not making a mistake by asking her to take on this life and my problems."

She stood and touched his face. "You're asking her to be by your side. Throughout history, every successful male leader has had a remarkable woman by his side. And of those women who have chosen to stand behind their mates, you can rest assured they've given their husbands a few swift kicks in the arse for good measure."

Marc grinned. "I've always wondered why my father looked as though it sometimes pained him to sit on the throne."

He held out his hand and drew her into an embrace, thankful to have rediscovered his mother's love—a love that had always existed. He'd simply been reluctant to accept it.

"Love well, my son," she whispered. "There is no greater power on this earth."

Marc kissed her cheek, realizing that what she'd said about love was patently true, and his love for Kate propelled him out the door and to his office, with Nicholas following behind him.

Once in the study, he told Nicholas, "Find Brigante and tell him to meet me here immediately."

"Are you calling a press conference, sir?"

"I am certainly not planning a ball, Nicholas."

"And when will this take place?"

"This afternoon, if all goes well. And I'll need your assistance."

Nicholas bowed. "As always, I am at your service, Your Majesty."

"Your Majesty? Are you getting soft on me, Nicholas?"

"Why, of course not. I will address you as I see fit, depending on what you are planning to do."

"Meaning?"

"If your plans include marriage to Dr. Milner, then I will address you as you so deserve to be addressed, Your Wiseness. And if they do not, then I will have to address you as Your Foolishness."

Marc scowled. "Were you listening in on my conversation with my mother?"

"I am appalled that you would think such a thing. I am only relying on my observations."

"Good."

"However, I do agree with your mother on the point of having a good woman by your side, and I must say that Dr. Milner is the crème de la crème of women. You could not do better."

"Thank you, Nicholas, for your counsel. And if you are quite finished with your commentary on what you did not overhear, I will tell you what I expect from you in the next few hours."

In the next few hours, Marc's life was about to take a turn. And if it spiraled out of control, he would welcome Kate as his anchor. He wanted her in his life, in his bed. As his wife, his life partner.

He wanted her more than he wanted the crown.

And damn anyone who told him he could not have her.

Kate would give anything if Nicholas hadn't interrupted. Marc had been about to say something. He wanted her to stay because… He liked the way she looked standing by a stove? He liked having her around for a little slap and tickle when the spirit moved him? If she went back home, would he even miss her?

She considered what she would be giving up if she did decide to leave. She loved her job. She loved Cecile as if she were her own child and Mary almost as much as she loved her own mother. And she definitely loved Marc.

Of course, the big question was—did Marc love her? If not now, could he ever love her? She could darn sure try to convince him that he could. And she would, even if he was the most stubborn, headstrong, sexy, to-die-for man she had ever known. She'd never backed down to challenge before, so why start now?

If Kate could have one wish, at the moment she would wish she were two people. One available to take care of her responsibilities, the other available to go after Marc.

Fifteen patients down, one more to go, then a long night of decision-making ahead of her. A lot of hours to choose between responsibility to her life's work and responsibility to her own life. If Marc ended their relationship completely, she wasn't as sure as she had been before that she could stand facing him on a regular basis, knowing what might have been. But she also couldn't stand the thought of leaving little Cecile or Mary. Or Marc.

Kate stopped in the break room long enough to indulge in a stale croissant and a cup of cold coffee, all she'd had to eat that day. Her appetite had gone out the door with Marc and hadn't returned because Marc hadn't returned. He also hadn't bothered to call.

Considering what he now faced, Kate couldn't blame him for putting her on the back burner. She didn't like it, but she didn't blame him. Hopefully, they would find a few minutes to talk, at which time she'd have plenty to say to him.

"Dr. Milner, I have orders to escort you to the town square."

Kate glanced from the beginner's French book she'd carried with her into the lounge to Bernard Nicholas, who stood at the door looking decidedly concerned.

And she was definitely confused. "Is there a medical emergency?"

"No, there is no emergency."

"But I still have one patient to see."

"That has been covered by Dr. Martine. This is of the utmost importance."

She stood, clutching the coffee cup tightly. "Can you give me a hint?"

"I have been instructed to say no more." He gestured toward the hall. "Now if you'll please follow me."

Kate started to issue a protest, but thought what the heck. Just another adventure in a long line of many. And maybe even the last one for a while.

After exiting the hospital's main entrance, they were immediately surrounded by armed guards, one in front, one in back and one on either side of Kate and Mr. Nicholas. And thankfully no press, unlike the last time Kate had dared to leave through the front door.

Instead of taking the car, they walked the four blocks in silence until they reached a mass of people and media members gathered round the statue of a white marble angel, her face turned to the sky, centered in the cobblestoned square. Mr. Nicholas motioned to Kate to follow him into an area cordoned off with bright yellow tape and protected by several members of local law enforcement. It wasn't until they had worked their way a few more feet that Kate glimpsed the makeshift platform. And standing behind the podium was the king.

Kate felt that old familiar longing when she looked at him. His neatly combed hair revealed his incredible face. His impeccably tailored navy suit enhanced his broad shoulders. His absent smile and confident stance made him seem every bit the monarch—until he looked to his left and their gazes met. Then she saw a fleeting glimpse of some mysterious emotion in his eyes before he turned his attention to the crowd.

He spoke in French and Kate could make out a few words, but not enough to understand what this was all about. She turned to Nicholas and asked, "What's he saying?"

"He's talking about the hospital and his plans for improvements." He waited a few moments then raised an eyebrow. "Now he's saying he's going to give away his car for auction with all proceeds going to hospital expansion."

"The Corvette?"

"It appears that way."

Kate couldn't believe he would actually give up his revered vehicle. "What's he saying now?"

"He's explaining the difficulties he's had with Dr. Renault and he's denying the threats. He does say that he dismissed the physician and he's giving his reasons for that decision. It's not very flattering."

Probably more restraint than Kate would have exercised when it came to Jonathan Renault. "Good. I hope they believe him."

At that moment, an attractive young woman walked to the podium and stood by Marc's side. As irrational as it seemed, Kate wondered if this might be some girlfriend he hadn't bothered to tell her about. Or maybe it was darling Elsa. But no, the woman wasn't a blonde, and she wasn't buxom. But she was looking at Marc as if he'd hung the sun hovering above them.

Oh, God. Was he about to announce his engagement? Had he chosen this woman next to him to be his wife? That thought halted Kate's breathing altogether.

She couldn't stand it any longer when Marc sent the woman a smile. "Who is that?" she asked Nicholas.

"That is Gabriella Collarde. The king is about to speak English and she will translate his words into French."

"Thank heavens. Maybe now I can understand him." Maybe now she could relax knowing this wasn't some paramour he'd been hiding in the palace broom closet.

"I would like to move on to the topic of the mysterious 'palace' baby," Marc began. "Her name is Cecile, and it has been rumored she is a DeLoria. I am here to confirm that she is."

Several people gasped, then a chorus of whispers ensued until Marc raised his hand to silence them. "All I will say at this time is she was conceived in love and she will be raised with love as my child."

He paused to seek out Kate and gave her his smile. "I would also like to publicly acknowledge another very special woman in my life—someone I've known for quite some time, yet it wasn't until recently that I've had the privilege of knowing her very well."

Kate locked firmly into his gaze. Her pulse fluttered and her heart pounded like a kettledrum from anticipation of what might come next.

"And if she would do me the honor of coming to my side, I have something I would like to ask her."

Stunned and absent of coherent thought, Kate turned to Nicholas. "Is he talking about me?"

Nicholas smiled. "He is certainly not talking about me, Doctor, unless he's suffered a severe loss of testosterone, which I greatly doubt. So I assume he does mean you."

Kate wasn't sure she could move; it felt as though someone had plastered her feet to the pavement. She definitely couldn't speak because a lump the size of a basketball had formed in her throat. And as far as her vision went, that proved to be a challenge, too, since her eyes were foggy with tears.

Had it not been for Mr. Nicholas's assistance, Kate would have stumbled blindly to the podium. But once they reached the platform, Marc reached for her, taking her hand and her heart as he helped her up the steps and pulled her close to his side.

When he turned her to face him and pushed the microphone away, it was as if everything around them disappeared—the masses, the mountains and even the clear skies above. Kate saw nothing aside from his cobalt blue eyes, his beautiful smile, his endearing dimples. She heard nothing aside from him saying, "I love you, Kate, and I want you to be my wife."

Kate opened her mouth, closed it, and opened it again, but the words wouldn't form around her threatening tears.

Marc looked concerned. "Do you love me, Kate?"

She sighed. "Yes. I always have. I always will. But Marc, I'm not royalty. I'm just…well…me."

He palmed her cheek in his large, warm hand. "And it's you that I want. You that I've chosen. The rest doesn't matter."

"It could matter to your people."

"I suppose we'll have to find out then." He pulled the microphone back into position and said, "I have asked Dr. Milner to marry me. Now, what do you think her answer should be?"

In many different languages, in many different voices, the word Yes! reverberated around them, growing into a chant that vibrated the platform.

He looked at Kate, his valiant heart in his eyes. "I believe you have their answer, and now I need yours."

When Kate didn't respond, he leaned to her ear and said, "One simple word, Kate. One big adventure. Together. Always."

How could she refuse such an ovation—or the man she loved with every solitary beat of her heart. "Yes."

Marc turned to the onlookers. *"Oui."* He laughed. "She said yes."

More cheers rose from the crowd as Marc drew Kate into his arms and kissed her without hesitation. A moving, tender kiss that Kate felt to the depths of her soul. After they parted, Marc smiled, Kate cried and Mary joined them, shedding a few tears of her own.

All three embraced for a moment and then left the podium together, Marc and Kate's arms around each other's waists. As the guards led them away, Kate caught sight of one cameraman with a white bandage spread across his nose. He moved a considerable distance back when they passed by him. Then someone called from the crowd, "Dr. Milner, what is your relation to the baby named Cecile?"

The crowd went deathly silent and Marc muttered, "You don't have to answer that," as he tried to move her forward.

"Yes, I do." Kate paused and turned toward the man making the query. "She's mine." Or she would be.

"Good show, Doctor Milner," Nicholas said from behind them.

Marc gave her a squeeze. "Very good show, *mon amour.*"

As Marc, Mary and Kate stood by the Rolls awaiting the return to the palace, Mary touched Kate's face with reverence. "I have always trusted my instincts, dear Kate, and I see they have not failed me now."

Kate hugged her again. "And I guess I have to learn to trust mine, too."

Mary smiled at them both. "You two go ahead with Nicholas. I have another car waiting."

"We'll see you at home," Marc said, finally feeling truly at home.

As he turned to Kate and studied her beautiful green eyes, he realized home had been there all the time, waiting for him to fill it with a remarkable woman with whom he could share his life, the good and the bad. The woman who had long ago rescued a prince from a frog before he had become a king. The woman who was worthy of bearing the title queen. His queen.

The woman who had taught him how to love.

Epilogue

Today, Katherine Milner DeLoria had become a queen.

Three months ago, she'd been common Kate, the doctor, but on this fair September day, she'd been set right in the middle of her very own fairy tale.

In a white horse-drawn carriage, bedecked with assorted flowers gathered from the last blooms in the palace gardens, she rode through the cobblestoned streets lined with villagers and the ever-present press, including television cameras capturing the event.

Maybe it hadn't been the royal wedding of the century, but to Kate, it had been everything she'd ever dreamed of—a white-lace wedding gown that had been worn by generations of Doriana's queens, a traditional ceremony held in the stunning, stone cathedral that had witnessed many a regal wedding. And most important, a gorgeous groom who could steal any woman's heart with just a look.

The atmosphere seemed surreal, dreamlike, but Kate's *hus-*

band—would she ever get used to that?—was so very real. Marc sat beside her with his left hand, sporting a wedding band, entwined with hers, the other lifted to wave at the onlookers who cheered as they passed. He wore a black suit, a gray striped ascot and a smile designed to please the crowd— until he turned it on her. It melted into a smile full of promise, of love, and Kate's heart melted, too, knowing it was only for her. Knowing he was hers for the rest of their lives, as he'd promised without hesitation during their vows. He hadn't seemed the least bit nervous during the ceremony—until he'd almost dropped the platinum-and-diamond ring he'd bought her in Paris two weeks before. But she could forgive him that momentary show of nerves. She could forgive almost anything, as long as she had his love.

When the coach stopped to allow the guards to clear the streets of some persistent reporters trying to best each other for the perfect photo, Marc leaned over and whispered, "You know something, with all that fabric you're wearing, I could slip my hand underneath your skirt and no one would know."

"I would definitely know," Kate said, imagining it in great detail.

"True, you would. Are you wearing those demonic panty hose?"

She grinned and shook her head. "White stockings held up by only a band of lace at the thighs."

He blew into her ear, exposed due to her upswept hair. "What else is under there?"

She shivered. "If you keep that up, King Marcel, I'm going to let you find out even if we are being watched on worldwide television."

"Damn the camera crews, but I suppose that might not be deemed proper, although very tempting. But just another mile or so, then we're off to Greece on a private jet, where we can do whatever we please, anywhere we please. The first order of business when we're airborne will be to get you out of that dress and those stockings and have some champagne, naked."

"Sounds like a very good plan, Your Studliness."

"Have I told you what I plan to do with that champagne?" he said as he again waved to the crowd, looking as if they were discussing the weather, not hot and heavy lovemaking.

Kate waved as Marc did, even though she really wanted to kiss her husband. Badly. "Do tell."

"I'm going to pour it all over your incredible body, and lick it off slowly."

She turned her face to his and brushed a kiss across his lips, the crowd cheering its approval. "And I'm going to do the same thing to you."

Marc groaned. "Could this procession go any slower? I'm going to die from wanting you before we begin our honeymoon."

Kate smiled. "If I remember correctly, we started the honeymoon last night when you showed up in my bedchamber even after your mother told you to leave me alone so I could get a decent night's sleep."

He raised a dark eyebrow. "Bedchamber? Spoken like a true queen. And I didn't hear you complaining last night. I did hear you moaning."

"Stop it or you are going to make my makeup melt."

He turned his attention from the crowd to her, surveying her face. "That wouldn't matter. With or without makeup, you're still the most beautiful queen Doriana has ever known, with my mother running a close second."

Kate sighed and squeezed his hand. "I'm going to need time to get used to being labeled a queen."

"The first gainfully employed queen in the history of Doriana, I might add."

Thanks to Mary, Kate thought. Her precious mother-in-law had insisted Kate continue her work at the clinic, even if

Mary had to go before the council and argue the point. Hopefully that wouldn't happen. The unrest involving the last scandal had finally died down after everyone had learned of the impending marriage between the playboy king and the common doctor. No one knew about Philippe and his wife yet, but Mary had promised she would write it all down and reveal the news after more time had passed. In the meantime, Marc and Kate would raise Cecile as their own child, eventually telling her about the way she had come to be. A story of love worthy of being passed down through the ages.

Marc leaned forward and groaned again, his attention now focused on an alley to their right. Kate followed his visual path and noted the reason for his obvious distress. A handsome young man sat on the hood of a black convertible, several young women fawning all over him.

"That's your Corvette, isn't it?" she asked.

Marc frowned. "Yes, and they're going to ruin the paint."

Kate fought a sudden bite of apprehension. "Are you going to miss the attention from all those women, now that you're a married man?"

He wrapped his arm around her shoulder and pulled her close to his side. "I'm only going to miss the car." He kissed her cheek. "I have the only woman I want."

"I still can't believe you gave up your car. Couldn't you have kept it and just given some money to the building fund?"

"Actually, I gave the car away to fulfill the terms of a wager."

"A wager?"

"Yes, with two friends from Harvard. We wagered that none of us would be married within ten years. If we did marry, we would have to give up our most prized possession. Although I did not adhere to the terms of the wager, I did last nine years."

"Any regrets?"

He touched her face with tenderness. "Only if I would have given you up. That would have been my greatest loss. I could live without the car, but not without you."

For the second time today, Kate was on the verge of tears. She willed them away and welcomed back the joy. "So have your friends married yet?"

"No. Mitchell Warner is living in Texas as a rancher."

Kate's eyes widened. "*The* Mitch Warner, from the Warner political dynasty? The senator's reclusive son?"

"Yes, that would be the one. Dharr Halim is a sheikh and his wife has been predetermined. But as of yet, he has not married."

"Are they here?"

"No, but Dharr sent best wishes and an intricate vase made by an artisan in his country, Azzril. Mitch sent a note that said, 'I knew you couldn't hold out,' along with a model of the Corvette. We're to meet again at a reunion in the spring." He discreetly moved their joined hands from Kate's lap to his thigh and slid it upward. "I'm certain they will understand why I could not resist you."

Kate understood only one thing at the moment—the way Marc was looking at her now, with unmistakable hunger in his eyes, made her want to tap the driver on the shoulder and tell him to hurry the heck up.

Kate glanced back at the carriage behind them that carried the queen mother, Cecile and her own mother and father. "I think my parents are getting along well with Mary. She's giving them advice on their tour across Europe."

"Mother enjoys that sort of thing."

"Honestly, I can't believe they're actually going to take a real trip. And when they return home, they're going to travel even more. When I lived with them, they wouldn't go anywhere or do anything. My mother wouldn't even get on a plane. I had to provide their entertainment."

"I can understand why they enjoy your company," Marc said. "I certainly do."

"Well, it's nice to have someone need you. To a point." Kate's parents had long ago crossed that point, but it seemed they had learned to live without her constant companionship, which was a very good thing.

He turned his serious eyes to her. "But I need you, Kate."

"That's different, Marc." With him, she had learned that having someone needing her didn't have to be stifling. "We need each other. And you do have a life beyond only me. We both have lives."

"We will continue to have a life together. That much I promise you."

"I know. But I also understand you have responsibilities." She batted her eyelashes in her best southern belle imitation. "Being as how you're a little old king and all."

Marc grinned. "There's that Tennessee accent I do love. I thought you'd lost it after learning French. I'm glad you haven't."

Kate rested her head on his shoulder and held his hand tightly when the carriage again lurched forward. "I could stand losing the accent, as long as I don't lose you."

Marc tipped her face up to meet his gaze. "You will never lose me, Kate."

She looked at him with all the love in her heart. "And I think it's wonderful that you've given up something you've greatly treasured for the sake of your people."

"You and Cecile are my greatest treasure. The three of us make a good team. And when she is older, we will have more children to add to our family."

Kate realized it was a good time for a few revelations, now that they were moving again, preventing him from jumping out of the coach. "Marc, there's something I have to tell you. Actually, two things."

He frowned. "Why so serious?"

"Because I don't know how you're going to feel about this."

"Kate, nothing you could say would disappoint me."

"It might surprise you, though."

"My life is full of surprises. You are a prime example of that. A very welcome surprise, in your case."

"Okay. Here goes." She drew in a deep breath. "Bernard and Beatrice are married."

"What?"

"I know. It's shocking."

Marc scowled. "When did this happen?"

"A month ago, in a quiet ceremony."

"Is everyone bent on keeping their marriage a secret in this family?"

Kate squeezed his arm. "Ours has been very public."

"True." Marc ran a hand along his jaw then looked at her again. "So I'm assuming that's all the shocking news you wish to tell me."

Kate chewed her bottom lip. "Actually, no."

"What else?" Marc asked, his tone wary.

"I'm pregnant."

His expression filled with awe as he laid his palm on her abdomen. "Are you certain?"

She rested her hand atop his. "Yes. I took the test two days ago. I wanted to wait until the right time to tell you. I figured this was as good a time as any since I have you captive in a coach, in case you decided to run."

"I promise you I'm not going anywhere." He proved it by taking her completely into his arms and kissing her deeply, thoroughly, eliciting a few whistles and catcalls from the crowd. When they parted, he told her, "You have blessed me twice today, Kate. I hope it's another girl, a sister for Cecile. I admit I favor girls. Much less trouble than boys. Ask my mother."

Kate was buoyed by his optimism, his love. "If we have a boy, I want him to be just like you."

Marc brought her hand to his lips. "I want him to be better than me, Kate. I want him to have your spirit, your strength."

"Marc, how can you say that? You're the strongest man I've ever known."

"You give me strength, Kate, through your love."

"And you do the same for me."

Kate recalled what Mary had said to her in the garden not long after she'd arrived in this beautiful country—to find a place in the world with this beautiful man.

I wish for you that kind of rare and precious love, my dear Kate.

Mary's wish had been granted, and so had Kate's. The consummate playboy had been replaced by the consummate king. The ultimate friend, an accomplished lover, the best father a child could know—loved her with all he had to give.

Truly a man for all seasons, and Kate's husband for all time.

* * * * *

Don't miss the exciting continuation of
Kristi Gold's miniseries
THE ROYAL WAGER in Desire.
UNMASKING THE MAVERICK PRINCE
(SD #1606) Available September 2004

Reader favorite

Eileen Wilks

presents

Silhouette Desire from *his* point of view.

MEETING AT MIDNIGHT
(Silhouette Desire #1605)

Seely Jones had secrets, hidden talents, a shadowed past.
And Ben McClain was fascinated by the elusive earth
mother who cared for him by day—and the fiery
temptress who haunted him at night....

Available September 2004 at your favorite retail outlet.

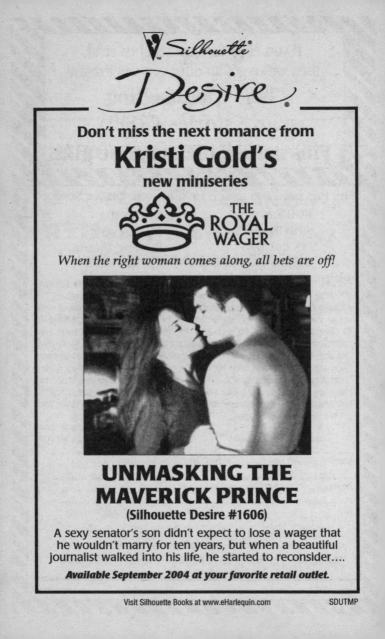

DYNASTIES: THE DANFORTHS

A family of prominence...
tested by scandal, sustained by passion.

THE ENEMY'S DAUGHTER
by Anne Marie Winston
(Silhouette Desire #1603)

Selene Van Gelder and Adam Danforth could not
resist their deep attraction, despite the fact that their
fathers were enemies. When their covert affair was
leaked to the press, they each had to face the truth
about their feelings. Would the feud between their
families keep them apart—or was their love strong
enough to overcome anything?

Available September 2004 at your favorite retail outlet.

COMING NEXT MONTH